Claude de Passioné.

The Precipice Between Love and Greed

A Claude dé Passione Novel

Claude de Passioné Series. Book 4

A Novel by John H Gray

Acknowledgments

The writing of 'The Precipice Between Love and Greed' was a challenge, and I thank the people who graciously gave their time and comments. I wrote this book while in several different locations…Aruba (my home), Quebec, Edmonton, Alberta, Canada, and Auckland, New Zealand.

I thank Barbara and Lissa Gray for their valuable input and criticisms. I also thank Denis Ricard for his good-natured comments and input, and for allowing him to be the fictional character in the story as the French Cultural Attache at the San Francisco Consulate, with the French interests in the Pacific, including Tahiti, as his responsibility. Appreciation to Guylaine Faubert for assistance with finalizing the manuscript. Leslee and Howard Tanasiuk for persevering and reading the drafts.

I also wish to thank you, the readers, for your comments and encouragement in writing the Claude de Passioné series of books.

John H Gray

www johnsnovels.com

May, 2025

Other works by the author:

Novels

Journey of Betrayals

Journey to Unknown Consequences

Rosita's Way

Claude de Passioné

Revelations and Peace

Life in Paradise Interrupted

Children's illustrated books:

English

The Adventures of Tutu and Tula: Lost

The Adventures of Tutu and Tula: Friends

The Adventures of Tutu and Tula: Christmas

The Adventures of Tutu and Tula: Rescue

The Adventures of Tutu and Tula: Brave

The Adventures of Tutu and Tula: Farewell

Wild Willy'sBreakfast Adventure

French

Les aventures de Toutou et Toula.........Perdu

Les aventures de Toutou et Toula.......Noel

Activity Books

Color My Aruba

Chapter 1

Rarotonga Airport. Private Lounge.

Rays from the early morning sun shone through the expansive glass windows of the airport's small private flight waiting area, filling it with harsh, bright light.

Claude de Passioné sat, dejected, thinking of the past few weeks and his disillusionment with life. If anything, his life should be one of content. It was not.

He reflected on how his life had progressed since his early childhood. The days he spent playing and exploring the vast vineyards in France that were owned by his aristocratic and wealthy family. He had loved imagining wild adventures as he played amongst the expansive acres of vines, and when he hid with friends amongst the barrels in the old wineries. He smiled as he recalled his first kiss with the local vicar's daughter and the excitement that followed as they explored each other's bodies. He decided those days were the ones that had sculpted his life experiences.

His quiet reminiscence was interrupted by the arrival of several other passengers destined for Tahiti on the small commuter plane.

An attractive Polynesian woman dressed in a flight attendant uniform, and wearing a freshly cut frangipani and hibiscus corsage, entered carrying a small case. She smiled at the assembled passengers awaiting the flight and addressed them.

"Good Morning. My name is Nalani. Our flight will be leaving on time this morning, and the Captain is expecting a smooth trip to

Papeete. Can I offer anyone a freshly made fruit juice or French Polynesian coffee brewed with beans grown on our local plantations? It is delicious!"

Light chatter drifted from the small group. Soon, cups of coffee were held in the hands of the passengers. A large tray of freshly made croissants was offered around by Nalani. Appreciative smiles were in abundance.

An older woman with an Australian accent asked Nalani what her name meant in Polynesian. The attendant laughed before answering.

" It means 'Serenity of the skies', which is appropriate given my job."

Her response drew polite laughter. Claude was pleased to sense the lighthearted mood among the passengers. When deciding to leave behind Rarotonga and the past week's deceit and heartbreak, he had feared that departing the island would be a painful and depressing event. The mood in the small waiting area elevated his otherwise gloomy mood.

He stood and walked to the small table to pour himself a juice, and arrived at the table simultaneously with a young brunette. Claude stood back and motioned for her to proceed before him in choosing a coffee or juice. She turned with a huge smile and thanked Claude. He was immediately enraptured by the intensity and beauty of her piercing eyes and long auburn hair. Her look left him breathless. He took a fresh pineapple juice and returned to his seat.

Minutes ticked by, and Claude found himself casting glances at the woman. He was admiring her when suddenly she turned and returned his look. She again smiled. It was a long and lingering smile, laced with the hint of an invitation. Claude's curiosity was triggered. He wondered whether he should approach her, given what had just transpired in Rarotonga.

To appear disinterested, he aimlessly read the wording on his boarding pass and ticket, as if he had just discovered it contained an error. He feigned concern, and by doing so, disguised his interest in her.

Minutes passed, and again he found himself watching her. Something in his mind was awakening and triggering a faint memory of having met her before, but he had no recollection of when or where that had been.

While Claude was trying to recall who she was, or the circumstances under which they may have met, the Captain and First Officer entered the passenger lounge, dressed in navy shorts and wearing short-sleeved white shirts with their rankings displayed on the epaulets. Four bars for the Captain and three bars for the First Officer. Nalani immediately went to them with coffee. Smiles and cheery banter erupted between Nalani and the Captain.

Claude was pleased. It seemed as if the mood for the flight was conducive to a trouble-free trip.

Chapter 2

Airborne

The flight departed on time after the passengers had filed from the lounge and walked the short distance across the tarmac to the shiny new Gulfstream II plane.

The climb out of Rarotonga was steep as the pilot accelerated the aircraft to clear the mountainous terrain and reach a smooth high altitude where fuel efficiency was optimum.

The engines whined loudly as they labored under power. Claude thought of the many departures he had experienced when flying on the family business private jet. He closed his eyes and again, his thoughts drifted back to his time spent at the de Passioné headquarters located at the sprawling vineyards in France. His decision to return to the family business had not been an easy one. Years earlier, he had decided to lessen his involvement with the business and leave the operations to his best friend and business associate, Barry Jones. It had proven to be a wise decision. The banks, shareholders, and family were astounded at the gruff Australian's success with the wine business.

Claude had met Barry Jones one evening at a local wine bar not far from the family vineyards in France. The rough and tumble Australian had engaged Claude in some friendly banter, challenging him to a friendly argument about his prowess as a vintner and the experiences he had when working at several award-winning Australian wineries. Claude had struck up a friendship that had blossomed over the years. Claude had hired Barry to assist after Claude's father, the Marquis, had been stabbed to death by the jealous husband of the Marquis's then-lover. As an insatiable womanizer and philanderer, the Marquis maintained many intense relationships throughout Europe. Many of his lovers were attracted by the extreme wealth and prestige of the de Passioné family. Those lovers' beliefs and desires would never be fulfilled.

Claude felt a pang of guilt. He had not told Barry of his current plans. He had left Barry in Rarotonga to clean up the shattered family mess. He wondered whether his bond of friendship with Barry would endure the abandonment of his past life and those who depended on him, including Peace, the daughter whom he had only recently found out about. His partner had fled from their relationship and had hidden for years. Her betrayal in hiding her existence had shocked him. His discovery of a 4-year-old daughter, coupled with his partner's devious actions to prevent him from ever discovering her, had driven a spike of distrust between them. He had loved his partner, Atarangi, more than anyone he had previously met, and he had intended to remain on the island of Rarotonga with her and leave the operation of the family business to Barry Jones. She was to be his lifelong partner. He had tried to forgive her for hiding the truth about Peace for all those years. He had written long, emotional letters to her while he was traveling on business. Theirs had been a brief but intense relationship when Claude had first visited the island. Claude had no idea at the time that the romance would swirl him into another life where he wanted to leave the rush of life in France and America. He was immersed in a deep, passionate love with Atarangi.

His thoughts returned to his family. There was no way he envisaged his mother, Marie-France, assuming any active role in the business. Initially, he had despised his mother. He hated her eccentricities. In his younger days, he had watched the steady stream of boys and young men visit the palatial old estate to satisfy her lustful needs.

Marie-France was a well-known character within society in France. Her eccentric ways extended beyond her interest in younger men to bizarre events and dressing in the most ludicrous combination of fashions.

In recent years, her behavior had been tamed somewhat after she met the wealthy Buzz Kutz. Buzz had inherited his father's industrial complex, producing components for IBM, GE, and other major corporations. Like Marie-France, he too had his share of weird values.

The true background of Buzz had recently been exposed during the kidnapping and smuggling crises in Rarotonga. Neither Claude, Barry Jones, nor any of their friends were aware of the undercover status of Buzz.

Young Claude had been thrilled to leave his dysfunctional family and enjoy a university education at the Sorbonne in Paris. His days at the Sorbonne included many extracurricular activities which drew the attention of both the University's academic masters and the French Gendarmerie.

Claude's attempt to secure part-time employment, to provide him with some independent money, resulted in his first introduction to crime and the law.

After graduating from university, and driven by a deep personal commitment and belief, Claude abandoned France and his family after announcing to his father that he had no intention of ever assuming a position of family control over the business. He set off to explore and experience the world, drawing on his massive trust fund.

Claude was jolted from his doze by a sudden pocket of turbulence that violently rocked the plane. The jet engines screamed as the pilot increased the thrust to take them to a higher altitude and bypass the disturbance.

The flight smoothed and leveled off. He looked around at the other passengers, and it was then that he saw the young lady from the airport lounge watching him intently. He gave her a little shrug and settled back into his thoughts. She smiled back a radiant smile and leaned across from her seat.

"Hello, I am Vicky Spagnoli. Have we met before? You look familiar."

Claude tried to recall. " You look somewhat familiar, but honestly, I cannot remember. Shame on me to forget such a beautiful woman."

Vicky smiled and pretended to be flattered. If only Claude knew her real intentions. " Are you traveling to Tahiti for a vacation or just transiting through to another destination? Not many flights from Rarotonga to anywhere other than New Zealand and some Australian cities."

"I am going to take a little time and visit Bora Bora. I have some planning to do and need the time to relax."

"What a coincidence. I am going to Bora Bora as well," she lied. Maybe I will see you there. What will you be doing other than work? Diving? Swimming?"

Vicky needed to contact her people on arrival to rush a reservation at one of the overwater huts. To impress Claude, they would need to demonstrate wealth. Given the power and ruthless reputation of her associates, arranging the best accommodation with no warning would not be a problem.

Vicky sensed that she was gaining his interest, and it would make him an easy prey for her to entrap him in her web.

Claude felt a brief desire arise within him to engage her in a longer conversation, but suppressed the idea. He wanted some time alone while there, but considered that some female company for dinner and an occasional beach relaxation would be welcome.

" That would be nice. I will be sure to look you up and we can share some time."

"I look forward to that. I find it so lonely on these trips with no partner to share them with."

Claude returned to his thoughts in silence. He was trying to focus his mind on the days ahead and the actions he would take to regain a position of control of the family businesses. Over the years, the family bankers and advisers had diversified the family fortunes into areas other than the wine business. Claude wondered whether there would be a business in which he could take an active interest that would remove his memories of the many failed romances he had endured. He had concluded that an enduring love would never be his. His mind drifted back to the untimely death of his fiancée years earlier, when she was struck by the Volkswagen Combi Van driven by a young hippie girl. It had happened on the day he wished to propose marriage to her. His subsequent romances all lost their intensity and evolved into diminished sexual marathons filled with the intensity and passion of the moment, but with no redeeming attributes that could lead to a commitment and a lifelong partner.

Claude leaned back, and his mind drifted to some of those encounters. He was surprised to find himself becoming aroused at 38,000 feet. He smiled. He hadn't lost it. He wondered how, after the tumultuous weeks he had just experienced in Rarotonga, his mind could wander back to those days. He found his eyes drifting back to Vicky and lingering there, and desiring to know what passion she possessed.

Claude wondered whether he should attempt to find out more about her before the end of the 2 ½ hour flight. It was an easy decision.

"Excuse me. I am sorry to interrupt. Were you in Rarotonga on vacation?"

"Don't be sorry. I love chatting as I find these flights boring. It was a working holiday. I am a financial analyst for Tantamore Capital Finance Group, we are an investment banking and hedge fund management company with offices in the UK, Sydney, and New York. I am in the UK office. Sir Reginald Coxburn is the distinguished Chairman of Tantamore Capital and a real charmer. He is researching a special project and arranged for me to work remotely from Rarotonga, away from the possibly spying competitors. I must admit that working from Rarotonga had its challenges," she lied, though part of her comment was true.

Claude was intrigued. "You must tell me more when we get together in Bora Bora."

Chapter 3

Calabria. Not all is Gelato

In Italy, the heat of the late summer was intense. Families with the financial means had fled the humid and prickly heat and sought relief at the shore.

Luigi Fratti had irritably endured the past month's extreme heat that had stifled life in Calabria. His business had suffered as his 'enforcers' had encountered many of their 'policyholders' away from their homes or businesses. The loss of the weekly income he raised by providing these small businesses with protection infuriated Luigi. His men still provided the 'guidance and business consulting', but there were expenses to be paid. Still, he and his mobster friends were counting on the big fish he had planned. That would settle him for life. Luigi could envision a life filled with games of Bocce, exquisite travel, fine wine and food, and satisfying his lust for beautiful women, even though he had married Donna Romano, the most sought-after woman in all of Calabria. He was anxious to leave his life of crime and terror behind. He considered himself too old when he watched the younger generation in action. They did things that were unconscionable in his day.

Luigi sat next to the open upper window of the family villa. Barely any breeze blew in to cool him.

"Donna," he shouted and waited. Minutes later, Donna entered his rustic office. She knew never to enter the sanctity of his office unless she was invited. In the early days of their tempestuous marriage, she had learned the hard way and still carried a small scar on the bridge of her nose.

"Luigi, my *caro,* you called me."

"Yes, please bring us something to drink and cool off. This heat is killing me. This afternoon I will not work. We will enjoy some wine and then we will bed. It has been too long since I savored your sweet ways."

Donna stood and left to find and fill a carafe with some of his favorite chilled wine. She returned and set the carafe and glasses on the small wooden table next to his desk and then poured the wine.

"Come, Donna. Sit with me on the divan. I want to talk to you."

Obediently, Donna walked to the couch carrying the glasses of the cold white pinot. She slid herself down beside him and marveled at how sweet he could be, yet she knew his reputation among the men of their village. He was both respected and feared. It seemed he was feared more than respected.

"Donna, we will take our daughter Maria and go to The Riviera dei Cedri (Citron Riviera) and escape this heat. There are some beautiful beaches for you and Maria to enjoy. We will take our maid, Bianca. She works so hard and deserves a holiday. Besides, we can afford it."

Donna knew that Luigi was having a torrid affair with their housekeeper.

"That is an excellent idea. Bianca certainly deserves a break from all she has to do here in this huge villa."

Luigi slightly frowned at the affliction and sarcasm in Donna's response.

"Donna, why are you being sarcastic? Bianca works hard. She comes from a good Catholic family. Why are you acting that way toward her?"

"Luigi, you must think I am blind and crazy not to see the looks and interaction between the two of you. She rushes to your requests but takes her time to assist me or others. There are hours when she cannot be found. Am I no longer desirable since I gave birth to our daughter?"

Luigi's face clouded. "I should discipline you for such impertinence. You are my wife, not my consigliere. Now that is funny….a female consigliere."

"Donna, you are my wife. Bianca is a servant and a friend. It is you I desire to pleasure this hot afternoon. You are still the most beautiful woman in Calabria."

She slid up beside him and playfully slapped his chest.

"Luigi, you flatter me. Now you said we will go to the coast to escape this heat. Which beach do you want to visit? As you know, there are several excellent beaches. I do not want to go to one with lots of tourists. I want it to be quiet so the two of us can be alone without your business interrupting or other disturbances."

"My father used to take our family to Spiaggia di Riaci. That was many years ago, and I am sure that at this time of year and with this heat, it will be a little busy. There will be some tourists. If it is too busy, we will drive and find other beaches. I will ask Vito to prepare the yacht and take us sailing away from the beach if there are too many people there. We will go for two weeks."

Donna was thrilled at the idea of time away on the coast and away from continual visitors to the villa, some of whom were known to her and others who were strangers, always coming to the villa in search of Luigi and asking for his time.

Luigi turned his gaze to her face, dropped his head onto her shoulder, and started nuzzling her neck. The intensity of the moment increased as he kissed the nape of her neck and proceeded to undo the ties at the back of her blouse. Her clothes started to fall away from her body, and he moved closer, holding her. Her creamy white breasts fell from the open blouse as he moved his hand down to her pudenda. She pushed back against his chest and, in an instant, ripped open his loose shirt, exposing his muscular chest. She dropped her hand to his belt and with minimal fumbling released his erect and swollen penis. Smiling, she raised her leg and straddled him. The lovemaking was long and intense. Finally, she groaned and then whimpered in ecstasy and collapsed beside him. He lay spent with lines of perspiration framing his handsome face.

"Damn you, Luigi. I wish I hated you, but I can't. I guess that makes me as bad as you."

Together they lay quietly and then slipped into a deep sleep, only to be awoken by the jangling of the old telephone in the Villa's bedroom. Luigi groaned and ignored the sound. The phone stopped ringing after some time, only to start again after what seemed like a long time.

"Someone is desperate to reach me. Why today and at this time?"

Luigi picked up the phone. "Pronto."

His face hardened and he balled his fists as he listened intently to the caller. No words were spoken. After several minutes, Luigi hung up.

"I think we should leave for the beach immediately."

"Is there something wrong? You look worried."

"I have told you before not to ask about my business. Let us pack now, and tomorrow our little Maria can enjoy gelato and swim at the finest resort and beach. Not all is fine. Just a crazy calling me."

Donna knew it was time to be quiet. She also knew that the accelerated need to leave meant there was serious trouble about to happen. She had been there before. She had read his intensity.

Luigi stood at the top of the stairs and called to Bianca, who came running to his command.

"Bianca, pack clothing for Donna, Maria, and yourself, as we are going to escape this heat and enjoy the beach and ocean. Pack whatever toys Maria wants." Donna turned to leave them. When she had left, Luigi continued, " And bring whatever toys we may need."

Bianca smiled, fully understanding his comment.

Chapter 4

de Passioné Estates. France.

Barry Jones was furious. The gusty winds and cold, snowy weather in France did not improve his mood. He had returned from Rarotonga through Tahiti and was aggravated when he checked into the Air France flight. The surrounding passengers were tanned and speaking excitedly of the adventures they had experienced. Barry's mood was dark and unappreciative of the other passengers' joviality. He had spent the week trying to resolve the de Passioné family mess. Marie-France had been difficult and attempted to coerce the authorities to allow her to remove Claude's daughter, Peace, and take her to France. She had tried legal tricks, claiming that Atarangi was an unfit mother and that she would be cared for better given the family's stature and wealth. The problem grew worse as Buzz attempted to call in his associates in the FBI and have them influence the situation. The Cook Islands authorities were having none of it, and the problem intensified.

Atarangi's brothers resorted to threats that were soon made by others. Barry sensed that they were approaching a point of danger. He demanded that Buzz take Marie-France from the island using his private jet. Initially, Buzz had objected, but soon changed his mind when Barry brought in her brothers. They had hurriedly packed to leave early in the morning.

Standing in his office watching a snow squall blast against the grape vines, Barry tried to understand why Claude had disappeared without advising him of his plans. It was unlike Claude. He and Barry shared almost everything.

Barry's frustration was further incensed by the reports he had received from the senior managers. He had left them in control while he was away in Rarotonga assisting Claude after the kidnapping of Peace had been announced.

 In the short time he and Claude had been away, a series of unusual things had occurred with the businesses. Barry needed to consult with Claude. There was no way he would attempt to discuss the business matters with Marie-France or Buzz.

Buzz had returned to find there were supplier issues. Critical bottling supplies were mysteriously unavailable. The bank with which the de Passioné family had banked for over a century was calling for an immediate audit and had placed restrictions on the business trading account.

Buzz made a call to the offices of the family Avocat to discuss the events. Monsieur Forget, the senior partner, had intercepted the call and advised Barry that a formal letter withdrawing their services had been sent a day earlier.

Barry walked back from the window and sat at his desk, trying to understand what had happened and how to proceed. He cursed Claude for his disappearing act. It was obvious the business was under attack, but by whom and for what reason was not clear to him.

In frustration, Barry looked at his watch and calculated the time in San Francisco. It was 5 pm in Paris, and the 9-hour difference worked in Barry's favor. He punched in the number and waited patiently until the receptionist answered.

"Good morning. It is Barry Jones calling from Paris on an important de Passioné Estates business. I need to speak to Delite Yeshi immediately."

Barry steeled himself for the anticipated reply. The wait seemed longer than usual. Finally, the receptionist returned to the line.

" I am afraid the partners are in a meeting with clients and will not be available for another hour."

 "What the hell do they think the de Passioné Estates and family are then? Tell that pontificating asshole of a partner to get his arse on the line."

"Sir, please don't shout and swear. I will try. Please hold."

Minutes passed, and eventually, the whiny voice of Delite Yeshi, the senior partner of Yeshi and Yeshi, picked up the call.

"Greetings, Barry. Good to hear from you. I am so happy that the whole horrible matter of the kidnapping of Claude's daughter is over. How is Claude? How are you? How can I be of assistance?"

Barry paused before answering. "Delite, this is going to take a while. I suggest you record this call, and after you review matters, send your best corporate lawyers to Paris. There is no doubt that the de Passioné family and businesses are under a very sophisticated attack. I must ask you why you delayed taking my call. Are you, or your firm, aware of anything?"

"No, not exactly, though there have been some rumblings and rumors circulating. It seems the kidnapping has created a lot of conspiracies out there. Let me ask our top corporate man to join us and then tell us what the situation is."

Delite left the room and returned with a lawyer named Horatio Henderson, who was also a forensic accountant.

"Barry, please tell us what has happened. We are recording your call."

Chapter 5

Italy. The CalaBrienCoast.

Luigi's driver pulled his private Maserati into the large sweeping entrance of the Capovaticano Resort Thalasso Spa.

 Donna, Maria, and Bianca followed in the armor-plated Mercedes behind Luigi's car. He was always on alert for any unseen attack and certainly did not want to compromise his family. He mused to himself that things like that never used to happen. He did not trust the young guys of today. He considered them unintelligent, fake mobsters. Luigi had chosen this resort to satisfy his wife's demand for privacy and no tourists.

Capovaticano Resort Thalasso Spa had a private beach. This made Luigi happy as he could station his men at either end to watch and guard the family and Bianca.

Luigi smiled. He had booked a spare room for his meetings and some discreet time with Bianca.

As the car pulled in and had barely stopped, bellhops rushed to the cars. Luigi's car was soon recognized, and the resort manager and chef waited to greet him in the resort foyer.

Luigi was not a man to be ignored or frustrated. The resort manager made a mental note to advise all the employees.

Donna and Maria were escorted to their room overlooking the private beach and ocean, while Bianca was shown a room in another part of the resort.

Luigi was pleased. His instructions had been followed.

The resort manager extended an invitation for the group to join him on the terrace for complimentary cocktails.

Luigi quickly accepted, but Donna, seeing her chance at revenge, requested Bianca to go and prepare the child's room as she would need to sleep early that night after her swim and all the car travel. Before Bianca could speak, Donna continued.

"Bianca dear, I am so fatigued. I will stay here with Luigi while you take Maria to the pool and then maybe a little walk on the beach. I am sure she is hungry, so buy her a gelato, but nothing else. The chef has promised a special dinner for us later in the evening. Maybe if Maria rests, she can join us for a while before you take her back and settle her for the night. I understand you will sleep in her room as there are two large beds."

Donna's bitchy comment was not lost on Luigi or Bianca.

Bianca attempted a forced smile, but it became more of a sneer as she turned and took Maria's hand.

"Come, dear. Let's leave the old people to recover. I am afraid they will not be much fun for you, but I will make your holiday exciting."

Luigi suppressed a grin. He was sure she would make him excited as well.

They sat on the terrace for over an hour chatting with the resort manager and enjoying the view over the beach to the ocean. A light breeze was blowing, and Donna welcomed the relief from the heat at their villa in the town.

Idly, they watched as Bianca threw a Frisbee to Maria, who squealed with delight when she threw it, and Bianca missed catching it.

They were still relaxing when a waiter approached carrying a silver tray. There was a folded and stapled card on the tray. Luigi took the card and carefully removed the staple.

The fact that the card was stapled was an indication to him that the content of the note was serious and not to be seen by other prying eyes.

He read the note and then stood to excuse himself.

"It seems there is some unfinished business back at the Villa. I must go and make a call. Excuse me. I will be back in minutes."

Suspicious, Dona turned and scanned the beach looking for Maria and Bianca. Neither was to be seen. Donna called the waiter.

"Can you please have both my daughter's and our room checked? She must have gone there with her Nanny to change and rest after the beach, but I want to check."

"Certainly, Signora."

Chapter 6

Papette, Tahiti Airport

Claude had chatted amicably with Vicky for the balance of the flight, intrigued by her career and finding he wished to know more about this astonishing woman. She seemed to embody all the attributes that Claude desired.

The plane touched down gently and taxied to the private arrivals area. Claude watched as Vicky gathered up her items and stood to exit the plane.

"Vicky, I enjoyed our chat, and since we will probably be neighbors in Bora Bora, I hope we can meet up and maybe you will join me for dinner and possibly a diving trip."

"I would love that. I will see you later in Bora Bora, as I need to use the business lounge here to contact my office. I will travel to Bora Bora later when I have completed a few things here."

Claude nodded. "I will see you then."

Vicky waited and watched until she saw Claude exit the arrival area and saw him proceed to the inter-island flight counter. She had carefully arranged a much later trip to Bora Bora by ferry. She figured this would cover any questions he may have about her delayed arrival.

When she was sure he was gone, she proceeded to the Business Lounge and flashed her Black American Express Card at the reception desk. She was quickly escorted to a private booth equipped with a laptop and phone.

Vicky checked her watch and then dialed the numbers she had received by text message on the secure and private service the group used. She realized she had to be very careful, as it seemed nothing was secure.

Her receiver buzzed with an unfamiliar ring. She could not identify which country the phone was ringing in. Finally, the call was answered.

Vicky looked around before she spoke in code. "Darling, I am in Tahiti. I have just seen the most beautiful scarf. I think you would like to see it on me. I want to buy it, but the store is closed and I won't be back at the airport for a few days. I need your permission to buy such an extravagant scarf."

The message was delivered. The scarf was Claude's, and the store being closed meant nothing could happen for a few days. The need for permission to buy was a code seeking the command to go ahead with what they had planned.

She heard a muffled chuckle before the click of the phone being hung up.

The mission was approved; had it not been, a voice would have come in on the call advising of the need to pay more for the call to continue.

Vicky felt an adrenaline rush and smiled. It had been a while since she had been in action herself.

Vicky walked out of the airport and flagged an old taxi to take her to a hotel where she could rest until the morning for the ferry to Bora Bora.

The driver screeched to a halt at the curb and jumped out, only too happy to have a fare. He jumped from the taxi and ran to place her baggage in the trunk.

The driver, named Sam, chattered nonstop to the hotel.

In the morning, Vicky purchased a ticket on the Apetahi Express ferry. She settled herself in for the 8-hour journey. She needed rest and planned to use the time for a nap and to plan the next steps to achieve her goals of detaining Claude and controlling the de Passioné businesses.

She found a relatively private area and set about arranging a sleeping space.

After buying some food and several strong drinks, Vicky settled herself in for the long trip. As she thought of the tasks ahead, she recalled Sir Reginald Coxburn's promises that Tantamore Capital would reward her handsomely. She was no fool, and if Sir Reginald Coxburn attempted to cross her, she had compiled a dossier that would put him away for life.

The ferry pushed back from the mooring at the wharf and slowly moved out to the open sea. Within an hour, Vicky had fallen into a sleep but had arranged a small device to drop and emit a loud, piercing signal if anyone attempted to interfere with her or her luggage.

She remained asleep until shortly before the ferry arrived at Bora Bora shortly after two pm.

The beauty of the island overwhelmed her. She had expected beauty, but this exceeded her dreams. She decided that when she retired, this would be the place for her.

A young boy ran to her, offering to carry her bags. He hoisted them and carried them to the shuttle for the hotel. She tipped him in US Dollars, and the young boy smiled in appreciation of the amount.

Chapter 7

Wall Street, New York City

Arnie Jacobson, the founder, principal, and CEO of the Arnie Jacobson Hedge Funds, swung back in the plush leather chair of his resplendent office on the 75th floor of the Financial Center. He stared out over the Hudson River as he watched barges being towed down the river.

He thought about the call he had just received and grimaced. He muttered to his junior confidant, "How dare that pompous British prick, Reginald Coxburn, Chairman of Tantamore Capital Group (UK), try to tell me how to manipulate things. He may have an association with the powers wanting this job done, but he forgets that I control the funds. No other company has such a large holding or control in the de Passioné businesses as my company. Without me, he has no influence."

He hit the intercom and called in his trusted junior.

"Abbott, check our holdings in one of his lesser companies. I think I will send dear old Reginald a little sample of what we can do. Pick one of the funds to collapse that has not been doing well, and one that is leveraged. Time for Reggie to sample what could happen if he steps out of line again.

And, get a leak out through our night traders. Order them to start dumping small amounts on different exchanges tonight, but increase the volume slowly. Once the activity starts, expect the analysts at the other firms to pick up on it. Get things underway before the day traders in the UK wake up. Get our friendly associate companies to start the process. I don't want any direct link back to our firm.

Reggie will crap in his British pajamas in the morning when he finds out what has happened. Unfortunately, I will be out with the boys on a fishing expedition in the wild. Contact Lillian and have her get my driver ready and get my buddies together so we can fly up to the fishing camp. Tell her to make sure we have all the supplies. I expect to be gone for several days. I will be unreachable up there. No cell service, except you will have my private sat phone number. How unfortunate for Reggie. Next time, he had better think smarter than to second-guess me and try things without consulting. The de Passioné deal is too big for him to single-handedly mess up. I am of a mind to contact the Italians and give them the news, but knowing Luigi and his hot temper, he may well decide to deal with Reggie the 'Italian Way' and no one would win."

Arnie hefted his heavy frame from the chair and stood menacingly in front of Abbott.

"What are you waiting for? The arrival of Jesus? Get on with it, man."

Abbott had seen this temper before. Arnie was not a man who leaned toward physical violence, as he held enough financial control over competitors and companies who served his purpose. So far, the authorities have not been able to pin any of the past market manipulations or illegal actions on him or the company.

"Yes, sir. I believe I have the ideal company in mind."

Arnie laughed and dropped back into his creaking chair.

"OK, who will it be?"

"Sir, our main fund has poured out money for the aircraft leases of that new Canadian airline. With all the Canadian government restrictions, we sheltered our exposure and brought in some investors from Sir Reginald's group. He had ownership in a few Canadian companies that met the Canadian government's ownership tests. The airline company is doing horribly, and our hedge fund investments are holding it together by allowing it to operate with the leases in default. The leases were arranged through an arms-length company we own. The leases are now millions of dollars in default, and given the airline's performance, they will never be paid. I will have the leases called immediately and rush through a bailiff's order to seize the aircraft. I will call our favorite judge to get this arranged. This was one of Sir Reginald's favorites. He had placed personal money into the airline. We only invested a small amount in the airline itself. We probably spend that amount on toilet paper in a month for the company. Our fund will not suffer. We still own the leases, and we have many others wanting to lease those aircraft. The shareholder investment in the airline company is nothing in comparison. This move is low-risk and an easy transaction to start. It was a brilliant move to separate the leasing arrangement from the airline's common stock. We are fully protected from the airline's failure."

"Abbott, you are a genius. I knew there was some reason I put up with you and your twisted ways. Reggie was big on that deal. I remember him bringing in his wealthy Canadian business friends to meet the strict Canadian government regulations. He was full of self-congratulation, and the Canadian and UK press carried extensive articles on him. I wonder how he will react to this event. I am sure it will cause an uproar. The Canadian government will lament the failure as inevitable, Reggie's wealthy investors will be crying for blood, passengers will have tales of woe arising from canceled flights, and the flight attendants and pilot unions will scream at the government. Oh, there will be some very entertaining days ahead."

Abbott smiled. "If you will excuse me now, I have some briefing to do with our traders."

Arnie grinned and contemplated the reaction of Sir Reginald Coxburn, who had invested millions of his family's money into the airline. He thought to himself, "I'm not vindictive, it's just a wealthy man's game, and I always like to win. Besides, the big prize will make everyone wealthy and more powerful."

Arnie settled down, and his thoughts then ran to the de Passioné project. The project was clever, huge, and required close coordination between the international partners. He was in awe of how Barry Jones had been able to take a centuries-old family establishment and direct it into the current times.

While Barry had gained experience with vineyards and wineries in his native Australia, he had realized that de Passioné Estates' growth was somewhat limited. He and Claude had successfully negotiated the takeover of other wineries in Europe and Australia, but the operating costs and logistics reduced profitability. Barry researched and convinced Claude and the investors to diversify. Barry quickly identified several distilleries and liquor distributors and brought them into a new company under the de Passioné banner. The company, Mondial, had flourished, and the ownership and financial incentives soon attracted other smaller companies to join the conglomerate. Within a few years, Mondial had branched out into the international market with its own directors and financing. The company had become a powerhouse offering many different brands of liquor.

Now worth billions, the company had become a darling for the initial venture capitalists and investors. It seemed the company could do nothing wrong or disillusion its customers. That would soon change.

Arnie thought through the plans and the members of the consortium who were instrumental in the project. He had concerns with the members and their interests, which were diverse. The Italians with money laundering and their drug trafficking network, the Chinese with the manufacture of drugs and their many drug labs, the British, and the funding smoke screen.

An unlikely marriage of sophisticated thugs.

Chapter 8

The Intercontinental Hotel, Bora Bora, Tahiti

Vicky was disappointed. Her request to stay in one of the over-water huts was not possible, besides, a hut would provide maximum privacy for the plans she had for Claude. It was the tourist high season and all were booked for months. Instead, she decided to stay where Claude had booked.

Claude had enjoyed the first 3 days of his anonymous stay at the Intercontinental Hotel. His days had been filled with snorkeling, sleeping on the beach, and relaxing in one of the hotel's luxurious tropical bars.

He had checked into the hotel using his anonymous ID as Jean-Pierre Simard. The ID had been made for him by the French authorities to allow him to travel incognito within Europe and not attract attention due to his extreme wealth. His given occupation on the ID was an undertaker from the extremely poor area of Seine-Saint-Denis, northeast of Paris. When the young women who were attracted by Claude's looks were told of his occupation, and he regaled them with stories of embalming corpses, they disappeared and left him in peace. Unfortunately, some seemed intrigued by his fictitious stories of reconstructing bodies that were grotesquely disfigured by crime or accident, or when he prepared a body for an open casket viewing after the body was returned by a coroner who had performed a deep autopsy. His occupation soon became to topic around the pool, and most tourists avoided him.

He chuckled as he thought about it and wondered whether he had inherited some of his mother, Marie-France's, eccentricities.

Vicky was exempt from his façade as she already knew Claude's real identity and history. She had discovered this while researching high-profile French companies. She had revealed this to Claude during the plane trip to Tahiti.

The fact that other eligible females avoided 'the undertaker' and left him alone gave her some satisfaction, as it made her job so much easier.

Lying on a lounger by the pool, Claude felt a strong sexual arousal starting. The surges were becoming stronger. He had experienced these several times over the past day and assumed it to be a sign that he was recovering from the trauma of the deceit and betrayal caused by his former wife and family. The last few weeks in Rarotonga had affected him greatly. He thought of his beautiful Polynesian partner, Atarangi, and the lies that she and her family had told him. He was still annoyed that they had hidden from him the fact that he had a daughter.

Claude was unsure if, or when, he would see the child again.

While relaxing, Claude snapped his thoughts out of the past and immediately started to think of the de Passioné business. He felt guilty that he had left Rarotonga without telling anyone of his plans. He had desperately wanted to be alone to gather his thoughts without anyone's interference. Now, however, his conscience was bothering him. He wondered how Barry was managing, but he was not overly concerned, as Barry had proven himself over and over to be more than competent in managing the business. Claude decided he would maybe call Barry later that day.

Lying in the warm sun, sleepiness blanketed him, and he drifted into a deep sleep.

Vicky had been inside the hotel, watching him from the pool bar. Seeing he was asleep, she decided to bribe her way into his room and continue her surreptitious actions. She smiled. Little did Claude know what she was orchestrating.

" Sir Reginald Coxburn had better be generous after all this," she mused.

Minutes later, and two hundred dollars lighter for the bribe to the housekeeper, Vicky found herself in Claude's room. The maids had the room made up perfectly. She walked to the bar and removed the bottle of Scotch with his company's deep purple and gold Mondial label. She had seen Claude drinking that particular brand at the hotel bar.

Carefully, she unscrewed the bottle. It was a new bottle and full. Concerned that the spike she wanted to add would overflow the bottle, Vicky lifted the bottle to her lips, took a long sip, and then poured in the contents from the small vial, replaced the bottle in the bar, and slipped quietly from the room. She hoped the GHB would work on Claude. She had read that GHB had previously been prescribed as a sleeping sedative, and she needed him drowsy and submissive. The dosage of the drug she used this time was larger than the previous doses she had slipped him, and yet undetectable. She planned to spike his drinks and food frequently and was relying on the GHB's effects to cause changes in his moods and desires. Little did Claude realize that his increased sexual arousal was the result of the small doses she had been able to add to the cocktails he had consumed poolside. She needed to be careful not to overdose Claude and had proceeded very carefully based on the advice of the drug courier that Sir Reginald Coxburn had arranged.

Vicky quietly left the room and positioned herself in the lobby where she could watch the guests entering or leaving the pool. She had a clear view of Claude still dozing in the late afternoon sun.

Claude's peace was shattered by a young boy and his sister, as she squealed in mock terror as he sprayed her with his plastic water gun. The stream of water missed the girl and doused Claude, his towel, and a book he had taken to the pool with the intention of reading.

Annoyed, Claude stood and gathered his belongings. Vicky watched as he walked towards the entrance. As he entered, she stood and walked to him.

"Claude, I was hoping to find you. I wanted to invite you for an early evening drink and then dinner."

Claude was about to decline the invitation, as he had planned to call Barry Jones that evening, but he took in the attractive brunette's voluptuous figure. She was dressed in tiny revealing white shorts and a fuchsia blouse knotted below her breasts and exposing her midriff, and white sandals with a heel that lifted her in a manner to display the curvature of her behind. Her look had the effect of accelerating Claude's already drug-enhanced desire. He considered his *chance* meeting with Vicky as fortuitous.

"I would like that very much, but as you can see, I am saturated after those brats soaked me with that stupid water toy. I need to go and change first. If you wish, come with me to my suite, and there I can mix you a pre-cocktail cocktail."

Vicky laughed and eagerly accepted. Claude's mind strayed to visions of satisfying his desire.

In Claude's suite, he offered her a cocktail and reached for the laced Mondial bottle. Quickly, she reacted.

"Oh, Claude. I cannot have whiskey as I react badly to it. I am a gin and tonic girl."

Claude grinned and continued to pour himself a large drink before
fixing her an equally large gin and tonic. He took a large drink
from the glass and excused himself to enter the bedroom and
change. Vicky saw the opportunity rapidly evolving. She was
ready.

Chapter 9

France. The de Passioné Estate.

Barry Jones tried to control his exasperation. Unexplained events were continually occurring at the business. Not only were the vineyards and wineries experiencing strange issues, but there was an exodus of some of the top managers at Mondial. It troubled him as there seemed to be no cause for their desertion. They were all paid well and shared in a healthy profit-sharing arrangement. When his HR department conducted exit interviews, none of them explained why or where they intended to work in the future.

Barry had spoken with a number of his friendly competitors, but no one could provide any information, and none claimed to be hiring any of the ex-employees.

Barry was stumped. He cursed and wished that Claude would at least show some interest in the business and call.

He was startled when the private phone jangled. Expecting it to be Claude, Barry snatched up the phone, only to be disappointed.

"Barry, this is Arnie Jacobson. I need to speak with Claude immediately."

"Sorry, Arnie, but Claude is travelling back from his island home. He has stopped on the way to take a brief break before returning to this snowy old France."

"Barry, I am concerned. Several rumors are circulating here. Seems Mondial and de Passioné are no longer the golden-haired favorites of certain trading houses. What is going on?"

"Arnie, I cannot answer that. Today, I met with several investment bankers. Earlier, they had requested a full audit. The audit did not disclose any peculiarities and shows a record profit and return on their investments. I am befuddled at what is going on. What have you heard?"

"Just some disparaging rumors about Claude. Seems the expectation here is that he is about to abandon the business. It will be broken up and sold off. Is this true?"

"No bloody way, mate. As we say down under, Stone the crows. No truth to that bullshit. I guess as one of our leading hedgefund investors you better get your arse out there and get that rumor killed, or you too will suffer."

Barry felt his temper rising and his patience with Arnie Jacobson shortening.

"Now, if there's nothing more I've got more important things to look after here than sit here discussing crap with you."

Barry slammed down the phone.

He was about to pour himself a stiff drink when there was a loud knocking at his office door. Exasperated, he went to the door and threw it open, about to explode at who was interrupting his privacy. A junior clerk stood with a larger old man dressed in a heavy winter coat.

" Mr. Jones. This man insisted on seeing you personally. He has a legal document ordering you to accept papers. He refused to leave the premises or hand the papers to me."

Barry eyed the man up. A bloody process server, he surmised.

"Hand me the papers. There is no point in playing any games. We have nothing to hide."

The process server leaned forward and, with a distorted smile, displayed his few remaining yellow teeth.

"Very good of you, Mr. Jones. I'm a bit disappointed as I expected some games from you. Was sort of looking forward to a cat and mouse game."

"Give me the bloody documents and get the hell out before I have you arrested for trespass."

Barry snatched the documents, spun around, and stormed to his desk, leaving the clerk to escort the man from the building.

At his desk, he ripped open the larger manila envelope. Inside were documents stamped with official court seals. Barry withdrew one and started reading. Within minutes, his shouting and obscenities filled the lower rooms of the house.

Again, there was banging at the door before it flew open, and Marie-France's husband, Buzz Kutz, rushed into the room.

"Barry, what the hell is going on? Your shouting and swearing can be heard throughout the house. What's happened?"

Barry shook a fistful of papers.

"This. It's a legal proceeding claiming that Mondial has violated and stolen patents. It names Claude, Marie-France, me, and several of the managers who recently quit Mondial as conspirators and the key guilty parties behind the patent infringements. This explains why we are losing good employees at Mondial. Who is behind all these problems? We have operated for years and never experienced issues of this nature. And, where the hell is Claude?"

"Barry, you and everyone else now know my past association with the CIA and FBI, after those incidents we just went through in Rarotonga. I could still ask certain agents to try a trace and see where Claude has gone. I assume he is probably using false papers by now."

"I think you had better find him. Things are getting serious and spinning out of control."

Chapter 10

Tantamore Capital Finance Group, Canary Wharf, London, England.

Sir Reginald Coxburn was pleased. He congratulated himself on his clever move to have Vicky trailed by his favorite thug, 'Knuckles' O'Brien, a ruthless Irishman with no scruples. He had met O'Brien years earlier while attempting to collect some personal debts owed by another prominent member of society. O'Brien had offered his collection services, and Sir Reginald was impressed with the results.

O'Brien had called him earlier in the evening to update him on Vicky's latest moves, including her accepting an invitation to Claude's suite.

Sir Reginald's dirty mind envisaged the erotic scene that he imagined would be happening. He was no paragon of virtue himself and had spent many hours at the hands of Vicky. He particularly enjoyed it when she tied the black leather dog collar with silver spikes on him, and walked him naked as a slave, all the while whipping him until he ejaculated. Just the thought of those sessions aroused him, and he decided he needed a refresher with a new madame he had discovered while attending a royal function. No one would possibly have guessed her occupation. He smiled as he recalled his surprise.

He stood looking out at the lights of London illuminating the night sky, content that the project was moving ahead as they had planned. Soon, it would be time to meet and finalize the arrangements with the Chinese and Italians. He shuddered as he instinctively trusted neither.

The idea of a meeting of all the parties involved concerned him. He had no trust in anyone, especially Arnie Jacobson. The Yankee Jew was a slippery bugger. Sir Reginald had kept certain secrets hidden from Arnie. There was no way Arnie could betray or perform a run around what they had planned. Always sharp and conniving, Sir Reginald had withheld certain key information.

His thoughts drifted back to the last trip he had made to New York and the meeting with Arnie. It was at that meeting, he met the Italian, Luigi Fratti. The link between Arnie and Luigi was never fully explained, but Arnie treated Luigi with great respect, even if it was false respect. The Italian wasn't smart enough to realize.

Efforts on the part of Sir Reginald to learn more about Luigi Fratti and his link to Arnie yielded little information. He had hired 'Knuckles' O'Brien to check Luigi out using his underworld contacts. O'Brien's contacts had been less than forthcoming. Many advised him to drop the investigation for his safety, but not before he learned of Luigi's control of a major drug trafficking operation and his links to other crime families across Europe, including the sophisticated network run by the Hells Angels.

He wondered whether the scheme that Vicky had devised regarding using the de Passioné businesses was wise. Sir Reginald was not one to have self-doubts very often, but this plan was complex and involved too many for his liking. It was too late for him to back out.

Still standing and reflecting on the situation, Sir Reginald decided he needed to establish strong alibis for his presence at other locations while the drama of the operations played out. He grinned as he thought of an ideal plan.

He called Lady Lydia Agnes Thwacker. Lady Lydia was one of the many who claimed links to royalty, and the cousin of Marie-France de Passioné.

Sir Reginald had escorted Lady Lydia to several high-visibility social events and had sparked a romantic liaison with her some months ago. He returned to his desk and phoned the private telephone number for Lady Lydia.

The shrill, high-pitched voice of Lady Lydia pierced through the phone. Sir Reginald grimaced.

Sir Reginald turned on his renowned charm.

"Lydia, my darling. I hope you are preserving that amazing beauty of yours. My heart sinks in your absence, and the loneliness is so hard for me. I need to see you. I have an invitation to the Royal reception for a distant Prince from Europe. It would greatly please me if you would honor me with your gracious presence on my arm at the affair."

He listened as Lady Lydia feigned surprise and hesitated, claiming she needed to check her social calendar. He knew it was a false stalling tactic.

"Reggie, my dear. I will need to turn down Sir Arthur Herrington Junior's party, but you come first. Of course, I will accompany you. I will need to visit the dressmakers and have a new gown made."

"I do not know how I will control myself. You are such a lavish dish."

Lady Lydia was no prude. "Reggie, stop it. You are making me suffer thoughts of the passion you have for me. Till then, my sweet."

Sir Reginald groaned. Taking her to the reception and being seen at such an event would establish his innocence while the others performed their sordid tasks. It was necessary, but he loathed the thought of spending the night captured by her. That was the price he would have to pay for his devious actions. Lydia Agnes Thwacker was as crazy as her cousin, Marie-France, and he wondered what crisis she would create at the event. He was sure there would be one.

Chapter 11

Capovaticano Resort Thalasso Spa, Calabria, Italy

Donna Romano was annoyed. The staff had located her daughter playing with some other children in the resort's children's center. Bianca was not with her.

Assuming that Luigi was with her in the other suite he had rented, she set off to confront them. She fully expected to find them in the throes of passion in the king-size bed.

Without knocking, she threw open the door with all her might. The door spun in and loudly crashed against the wall as it opened fully. The paintings of the coast and boats sailing the ocean on the walls swung and crashed back against the walls.

Donna stopped and froze in her tracks. Sitting around a circular table were 10 men dressed in suits. These were not vacationers. Luigi rapidly pulled himself up from his chair and ran to her.

"Donna, what is wrong? What has happened? Why have you burst in here? This is an important business meeting. Where is Maria? Is she alright?"

Complete silence filled the room, which reeked of cigar and cigarette smoke.

Luigi took Donna firmly by the arm and led her back out into the corridor.

"Don't you ever fucking interfere in my private meetings? Do I make myself clear? Now get the fuck out of here and go find that snot-nosed brat of yours," he hissed.

Luigi was shaking with fury. He had lost the prestige and control of the meeting in front of his mobster friends. Her intrusion had weakened his reputation.

Donna was equally infuriated, and her Latino temper flared higher as she returned to her room. She vowed right then to settle her score with Bianca. Her husband Luigi had enjoyed his last fuck with her.

Grabbing a bottle of Scotch from the bar, she sat on the bed and devised a plan to rid herself of Bianca. She quickly downed several glasses of the amber drink, and with each, a plan crystallized. In her mind, Bianca would not see the end of this day.

Suddenly, she realized that she had no idea where Bianca was. Maria was alone with those kids and the resort's staff member who supervised the play area.

Still angry and irrational, Donna left the room and proceeded to the casual restaurant overlooking the ocean. After ordering a seafood salad and a bottle of Chablis, Donna settled in and considered the available options to deal with Bianca.

She was in deep thought when a booming voice from behind startled her. Turning around, she found her former lover, Vito Colangelo, standing with a beaming smile. He had never accepted that she had left him, and continually followed her with a repertoire of promises and requests to win her back. He was one of the few who were not afraid of Luigi and had told her on many occasions that Luigi would never be found to disrupt their lives together if she went back to him.

Donna looked up at him. He was attractive in that distinct Italian way. His dark eyes were set alight by his golden-tanned face and shoulder-length black hair. He wore tan chinos and light-colored loafers. His pale cream shirt was unbuttoned, and several gold chains and a crucifix hung over his chest hair.

Donna reached out to him. "Vito, please leave. This is not a good time." Vito looked at her shaking hand and immediately concluded that there was indeed trouble. He pulled up a chair and, while holding her hand, focused a penetrating look into her eyes.

"I know you, and when something serious has upset you. What is the problem?"

Listening to his reassuring voice, Donna's eyes moistened. She told him of her interaction with Luigin and her hatred of Bianca. Vito listened attentively without interrupting.

"You should leave that bastard. I told you before you married him that he was no good for you. He treats you like garbage. Leave him and come with me."

"I am flattered that you still love me. You have been a good and loyal friend, Vito, but it is too late. Luigi will kill you if he knows you still want me, plus I now have a child."

"It is not too late. I can deal with Luigi. You will have nothing to worry about."

"No, Vito. I do not want any harm to happen to Luigi. He does look after me, but I know he does not love me as you did."

"Donna, what can I do to make you happy?"

"Vito, there is nothing. Maybe get rid of that Bianca bitch so he is not distracted by her."

Vito slumped back in his chair and stared at her without saying a word. Minutes passed by in silence.

"Vito, don't go and try anything stupid. Luigi is up to something big. That meeting had some Dons I recognized from other districts. There is something big planned. He will be guarded by his men at this time. It will be very dangerous for you to be seen with me or to approach him."

"He and his henchmen do not scare me. There are things you do not know, and I can assure you that Luigi Fratti will never threaten or try anything."

Donna frowned. "Vito, did you know I was here, or is this an accidental meeting?"

"It is best some things are not discussed."

"But how did you know I was here at this resort and here in this restaurant? I chose this location to be private and away from the eyes of other guests."

"Donna, I have some of my best men working here. They are my eyes and ears."

A family, obviously on vacation and having just arrived at the resort, rushed past them to view the beach. The kids shouted and ran down the stairs to the sand.

Vito grasped her hand a squeezed it. He stood and bent over her and kissed her fully on the lips.

"Ciao for now. I will see what we can do to make you happy."

She watched as he walked away, admiring his handsome physique and wondering whether she had made a mistake in marrying Luigi.

The afternoon dragged by. Donna dozed off, and when she awoke, it was late afternoon. She panicked, and after leaving her room information for the waiter, rushed to retrieve Maria from the play area. It was still busy. Maria was riding a bouncy ball and laughing with a blonde boy. Donna called Maria, who came running across to her. Donna thanked the assistant and tipped her. The assistant marked Maria off a chart, and Donna turned away to walk back to the room. As she walked through the garden and back toward the reception area, she heard loud cries and shouting. Donna stopped and turned in the direction of the shouting and walked toward it. She arrived at the resort's hot pool, which was set amongst the lush gardens. A crowd of people dressed casually was pointing and shouting. Several resort employees in uniform were running to the pool, and one jumped in fully clothed.

Donna pushed through the front. She looked and saw a body floating face down in the pool. Instinctively, she placed her hand over Maria's eyes and led her away.

Across from the pool, she saw the group of men that Luigi had been meeting with. Luigi was amongst them. He stared with a look of hatred at Donna. She looked away and noticed Vito Colangelo standing off to the right of some short bushes. He saw her looking, smiled, and then shrugged before turning away.

Bianca Barbieri was dead.

The distinctive wail of the sirens of the Carabinieri cars shattered the quiet of the beach area. The cars screeched to a halt, and uniformed officers ran through the grounds.

At the site of the arriving police, Luigi's business partners dissolved into the crowd and disappeared.

Chapter 12

de Passioné Estate, France

Barry Jones recalled the last few days he had spent talking with Claude before departing Rarotonga. In front of him on his desk, he had arranged a chronological chart showing the dates of the various defaults and demands placed on the vineyard by creditors and suppliers.

He tried to remember whether Claude had mentioned anything regarding any of them. He drew a blank. Frustrated, he left his office and walked to the salon where his wife, Yvette, sat in conversation with Marie-France. Barry was not in any mood to accommodate Marie-France's antics, but on seeing her and her choice of clothing for the evening, he could not suppress his laughter. Yvette looked daggers at him.

Marie-France was holding an antique gold goblet. Her hair had been dyed bright orange, and a small silver tiara crowned the mass of artificial curls. Barry conjured up an image of an orange-haired Statue of Liberty. She wore a long, bright purple kaftan. The bodice was decorated with bleached wooden beads. On her feet, she had on fluffy pink lambswool slippers.

Yvette smiled up at Barry. "Marie-France is feeling very special tonight. She received a call from her cousin in England this afternoon. Her cousin, Lady Lydia Thwacker, is coming to visit. Her cousin is related to royalty in Britain."

"Good lord," Barry thought to himself. "Just what we need with all the problems here at present. Another crazy running amok in the house."

Yvette sensed his despair.

"It should be fun, Barry. She is coming with an old friend of hers, Sir Reginald Coxburn."

Barry groaned. Marie-France looked at him. "Are you not feeling well, Barry?"

Yvette was enjoying the situation immensely. She was trying hard not to convulse with laughter when she looked at Barry's face.

Barry turned to Yvette, "Dearie, could you do this old guy a favor and get me a glass of that overproof Mondial whiskey? I think I need it."

Marie-France continued to look at Barry, concerned he wasn't well, and missing the whole point. Barry sank into the large cushions of the oversized couch.

Yvette returned with the whiskey in a larger tumbler. She smiled at Barry, who had picked up on the larger-than-normal glass. He mouthed a thank you.

"So, Marie-France, when does the royal delegation from England arrive?"

Again, Yvette could not contain herself. She watched poor Barry's face as he readied himself for her answer.

"Next Wednesday, in the evening. I will arrange a special luncheon for Thursday."

Barry was halfway through swallowing his drink and choked at the news. He did not need any more distractions. The company was in trouble, and he had no desire to host anyone, let alone the pompous Brits.

"Will Lady Lydia and Sir Reginald be taking any tours?"

"No. It has been a long time since she visited. I am going to contact other members of the de Passioné family to come for a major party the following weekend."

Barry's jaw dropped.

"If I can ask? How long are they staying?"

" I believe at least a month. Oh, it will be fun."

Barry sensed a problem developing. He was aware of some link between Sir Reginald and Arnie Jacobson, but the full details of that link were unknown to him. He assumed that they had a relationship due to their respective involvement in the financial market. Barry had no idea of the common criminal activities of the two.

"Yvette, my dear. You and I will need to visit the fashion boutiques in Paris in the next day or so. I must be dressed appropriately for Lady Lydia and Sir Reginald."

Neither Barry nor Yvete was aware of the secret and lustful desire that Marie-France harbored for Sir Reginald. In her mind, Marie-France recalled the nights she and Sir Reginald had shared at the posh Savoy Hotel in London. Just those thoughts alone caused her to shudder at the thought of the possible upcoming liaison the three would share. She wondered whether Buzz would join in.

She snapped out of her remembrance of those days and her dream of what lay ahead when Barry cursed out loud.

"Bloody hell. Where the fuck is Claude? We need him here now. Instead of looking after the business, he is off cavorting with God knows what or who. I am pissed at him."

Yvette became annoyed. She considered Barry's outburst unwarranted.

"Barry, he has been through a terrible time in Rarotonga. The kidnapping of his daughter, then the exposure of the plot to deceive him, and finally the collapse of his marriage. I am not surprised he has decided to take some time away by himself. I am sure he is safe and living quietly while he emotionally recovers from those events. You must remember that Claude is only human. We forget that he has done a lot for the business and others. His life has not been simple. He has experienced more upheavals than most people. Claude has been a good friend and partner to you. He has given you opportunities that many others wouldn't. Is this reaction of yours because you cannot cope?"

"I can cope, but the issues I need to manage are strange. It would help if Claude were here. I need his advice."

Marie-France had listened intensely and, after reflecting on Barry's comments, replied.

"Barry, you will be able to discuss some of the business challenges with Sir Reginald when he arrives. He is a smart man. He has excelled in business. I am sure he will offer some good advice."

"Sir Reginald knows nothing of the wine business, plus he has been involved in some questionable things in his past. I don't want him involved in any of the de Passioné business, and certainly not in the Mondial Distillery business. I do not trust that man."

Marie-France looked shocked and felt a wave of anger rising in her at the suggestion that her friend and deviant partner were being criticized. She was about to explode at Barry when the front door system sounded to signal the arrival of visitors.

Barry was relieved at the distraction and excused himself to meet the visitor. He was pleased to find Horatio Henderson from their US-based legal firm, Goudge and Hammer, standing at the entrance.

Horatio was accompanied by a stern-looking woman and a shorter man.

"Come on in, Horatio. Your timing is perfect. I am sure you are tired after that trans-Atlantic flight, so join us in the salon. We are just having drinks and discussing some business. Who are these folks accompanying you?"

Horatio motioned to his traveling partners.

"This is our most senior corporate lawyer, Sylvia Piper. She has years of experience in forensic and corporate litigation. Her experience includes some major US and International cases. Joining her is research assistant Charles Snead. One of the best snoops in the business. While they will be working on your affairs here, resources in the States and London will be backing them up."

Barry nodded.

"Come and meet Claude's mother and my wife, then I will show you to the guest rooms."

Barry showed the trio into the salon, and introductions were made. After brief greetings were exchanged, Barry escorted them up to the guest rooms on the second floor.

"I will leave you here to freshen up after that long flight. You will find toiletries, towels, and a welcome ensuite shower. Take your time, then join us downstairs. I will have the kitchen prepare a light meal for you. Tomorrow, we will get you set up in an office at the winery headquarters."

Barry handed each of them a key and left to return to his wife and Marie-France.

Upon returning to the salon, Barry found Buzz sitting with the women.

"Barry, what is going on? Why do you have the firm's legal eagles here? Are there problems?"

"No, Buzz. There are some logistical issues with certain suppliers. We have had contracts in place for years, and now it seems certain political and financial issues have arisen. This is not unusual, but I need to ensure that de Passioné Estates and Mondial Distilleries are protected from any potential political or financial indiscretions. I wish that Claude were here. He has a deeper history with the business. I have no idea where he is. This concerns me greatly, as he has always kept us informed, no matter where he was traveling."

Buzz sat quietly for several minutes before answering.

"Barry, after the events that occurred in Rarotonga, you are now aware of my past involvements with the CIA and FBI. I still have deep personal contacts in those organizations. If you give the word, I will get them tracing Claude."

"I will consider that, but give it another day or so. Claude may have just decided to take time alone after the shattering experience of finding a daughter and losing his wife."

"Let me know. I will have him found."

Chapter 13

Intercontinental Hotel and Resort, Tahiti

Vicky watched as Claude slumped forward and then collapsed back onto the couch. His head fell against the cushions. His eyes were closed and his mouth slightly open. She had been concerned about using GHB on him. She was aware of it being a common date rape drug but had never considered it as a drug capable of rendering a fully grown and muscular man like Claude unconscious. Her contact in Tahiti had assured her that the drug would work on Claude and that the after-effects would make her planned goals easier to implement.

Vicky moved over to the couch and, after removing Claude's sandals, raised his legs onto the couch and moved his body into a fetal position. She had been advised that the potency of the dose would mean he would be knocked out for at least 8 hours.

She decided to use this time to contact her associates and report on progress.

The first call she made was to her partner in crime, Sir Reginald Coxburn. She ignored the time difference between Tahiti and London. She didn't care and assumed Sir Reg would probably be satisfying his obsessive sex needs with some cheap whore. She punched in the numbers for his untraceable private satellite phone.

The chirping tone continued, but the phone went unanswered. Vicky cursed and assumed he and the whore were probably passed out from partaking in some heavy drugs. Annoyed, she considered the need to replace Sir Reg as a partner. He was becoming sloppy and a liability.

Her thoughts were ended by a shout from Claude. She spun to look at him. He was still unconscious but talking and calling out in his sleep. Vicky was startled and concerned that his voice would be heard outside the room. She rushed to the flat-screen TV and flipped it on. She surfed through the channels until she found a music channel and turned it loud. Claude's incoherent ramblings were drowned out by the music.

The first part of her plan was going to accord. To proceed, she needed to contact the local drug dealer whose information had been provided to her before she left London. She hoped the information from her London source was safe and accurate.

After checking the time, Vicky called the local number provided. The phone was answered by a man with a heavy French accent. Vicky identified herself and made arrangements for the man, or one of his gang, to deliver a package to the hotel. An amount was agreed upon, and the call ended.

With Claude passed out, Vicky sat thinking of the situation and the events that had brought her to Tahiti. She recalled her past and how she arrived in this situation.

Years had passed since she had started at Tantamore Capital in London. She had left her family's impoverished farm in Calabria. Like the other neighboring farm families, life had been hard. Food and the necessities of life were available, but there were no extras. Vicky attended a public school where she saw other children from wealthier homes enjoy things she could only imagine owning. Throughout her school years, her desire for wealth grew and became insatiable. There were times when the teachers searched the children and scorned them when theft occurred. Vicky was smart, and the ill-gotten items were never discovered. Her family watched in dismay as Vicky grew from a charming young daughter to a fierce and aggressive teenager. She grew to despise her father and criticized him for their poor financial state, ignoring his lack of training and equally poor upbringing. Vicy was determined to never be poor or want anything.

At age sixteen, looking much older, she disappeared one night from the farm. She headed to Lamezia Terme, where it was easy to find travel to other locations in Europe, America, and England.

Desperate for money, Vicky lied about her age and was hired to work in an old bar near the disused pier. She befriended some of the men who worked on the construction of the airport and soon selected one as her lover. Her choice was fuelled by his plans to move to London. Falsely, she professed her love and agreed to travel to London with him. Shortly after they arrived in London and found a flat, Vicky again disappeared. This time it was with a somewhat socially deficient accountant. He was enthralled to have an exotic Italian woman and worshipped her. She attended boring accounting parties and functions, which is where she met Sir Reginald Coxburn. He was the guest speaker on taxes and investing. His speech bored her, but his wealth and social standing did not. He became her target.

Again, she disappeared, leaving the socially deficient accountant heartbroken and contemplating suicide. Sir Reginald tried to convince her to move into his mansion, but she insisted he lease her an apartment. She did not want anyone to know of her schemes.

Sir Reginald lavished her with gifts. After several years with him, she decided to pursue the project she had dreamed of. Over a romantic dinner at London's famous Dishoom Indian restaurant, she broached the subject.

"Sir Reggie, I wish to go home to Italy and visit some old school friends."

"My dearest, I am confused. You told me your family was deceased, and you had no friends left there. Why do you want to return to such a sad place?"

"I still have a good friend there. He was not like the others when we were growing up. I have stayed in contact with him and his wife. He has a good business and is very rich and powerful."

At those words, Sir Reginald's interest spiked.

"Why have you never told me about this friend of yours?"

"I saw an article in the newspaper last week, and it featured him. It brought back a lot of memories. Even though I stay in contact, it is not the same as visiting. Please, can we go?"

"I will need to consult with my staff and check my calendar. I am a very busy man. I cannot just leave."

"If what I read in that article is correct, my friend may become an important client for you."

Sir Reginald pushed his plate away and sat back with his fingers pointed beneath his nose. His interest level increased.

"I'm interested. What is his name and what is his business?"

"His name is Luigi Fratti. He operates some companies in the import and export business and has ownership in some investment firms."

"He sounds interesting. I will check him out. Now, let's go. I have a special plan for you tonight, and it's naughty."

"Reggie, you are incorrigible."

Vicky was snapped out of her recalling the past by a sharp rap at the door. She spun and looked at Claude and then cautiously went to the door and looked through the little security viewer. Outside was a bellman dressed in a white jacket and black trousers.

She quietly cracked the door open.

"I have a package for Miss Spagnoli."

Vicky accepted the package and reached for her bag on the table near the door. She handed the boy a ten-dollar tip. He smiled and left.

On the couch, Claude was stirring. Vicky quickly walked to her room and placed the package beneath some clothes in her suitcase. She knew the contents of the package and planned to use them to achieve her goals with Claude.

She returned to the couch and shook Claude's shoulder. He woke in a groggy state.

"Claude, the sun will be setting soon. I think you must have had too much sun. You fell asleep. It has been hours."

Claude tried to focus. His head thumped, and he was disoriented.

"Did I drink a lot? What happened?"

Claude looked at Vicky. He felt strange and found himself strangely attracted to her. Vicky smiled.

"Let me get you some water. Sit here and wait. I will return in a minute."

Vicky left the room and headed to her bedroom. In her room, she reached into her suitcase and removed the package the bellboy had delivered, which she carefully unwrapped.

In her bathroom, she poured some of the pink-colored Sildenafil into a glass of wine. She smiled, knowing the liquid Viagra would soon react on Claude in his drowsy state, and her intense seduction of him would start.

Chapter 14

de Passioné Estate, France

Buzz Kutz and Barry sat alone in the salon. Marie-France had left them to, as she put it, " Enhance my beauty" before the legal team from the US joined them.

"Barry, I share your concern. I have never known Claude to disappear like this. Have you contacted Atarangi or her family back in Rarotonga?"

"Yes, I called earlier. They have not heard from him, but confirmed with the resort that he had checked out early two days ago. They were unable to locate any taxi driver who may have driven him to the airport. He just seems to have vanished."

"No one just vanishes. Especially on a small island like Rarotonga. I will have my contacts check the passenger lists for all the flights that have departed Rarotonga since then. If he left on a plane, we will find out where he went. I do not believe he left the island by boat, but it's possible."

Barry sat in deep thought. He mentally traced back the other occasions when Claude had taken time alone to deal with personal issues. He recalled that every time, Claude had stayed in contact. This time, it made no sense.

"Buzz, before Marie-France returns, I should explain some things. There are too many problems arising in the business. Suppliers and creditors with whom we have dealt over the years are nervous. Some have withdrawn credit, and others will no longer supply certain products. We have adequate resources to last us for a few more months, but it will reach a critical stage in the next few weeks if we don't restock. The banks insisted on a forensic audit, and so far, there has not been any issue. What is happening is unexplainable. That is why the legal team is here. We need their expertise to determine why this is happening. I have personally spoken to the managers and owners of some suppliers. No one has admitted anything, though several seemed nervous when I asked about the issues. I received vague or no responses."

"Someone knows what is behind this. I suggest we make it desirable for that person to share some information. Maybe a little Cash might free up their tongue."

"I have offered a bonus based upon early and larger deliveries, but none of the suppliers were interested."

As they sat contemplating the situation, Horatio Henerson from the legal team arrived back in the salon.

"Tomorrow we will need to review some of the past transactions to build a picture of how things have been operating and to try and identify anything out of the ordinary. I suggest we start with the financial transactions, in particular, all the banking details. Payments to vendors and receipts for received payments. I will need them for all parts of the company, including Mondial, for the past year."

"Crikey, Mate. That's going to need all of our accounting staff. Going to take weeks."

"Well, Barry, we have to start somewhere, and generally these investigations uncover questionable transactions. My associates will also need access to personnel records, especially any related to employee terminations or problems. It may be necessary for Sylvia Piper to interview some of the staff."

"Bloody hell, Horatio. I don't want this investigation to start rumors and problems amongst the staff. Until your people have completed the financial part of the investigation, access to the staff is off-limits."

"I suggest, then, that our research assistant Charles spend some time getting to know the staff informally and see if he discovers any rumors circulating that could contain information about what is happening."

The conversation ceased when Marie-France returned. All heads turned to observe her entry to the room.

Marie-France, expecting to participate in the meeting, had dressed in what she believed was appropriate business attire. She had dressed in a tight black pencil skirt, red fishnet stockings, and a see-through blouse under which was a bright yellow bra. Her hair was teased up into a formidable beehive. Several heavy gold chains dangled from her neck.

Barry alternated between deep embarrassment and comedic relief at the sight.

Buzz, seeing the reaction of Barry and Horatio, quickly intervened before she could speak and do more damage to the serious discussion that had been taking place.

"Come and let Barry and Horatio stay and talk about the boring business things. You look so inviting, I want to spend time alone with you. It's a nice evening. Let's go out on the terrace and enjoy a nice wine before we retire for the evening."

Marie-France batted her eyelashes at Buzz and feigned an embarrassed smile.

Shortly after Buzz and Marie-France left, Sylvia Piper and Charles Snead joined Barry and Horatio. Barry addressed the group.

"I had the kitchen staff prepare a late light supper for us. Let us proceed to the dining room."

Over the light meal, Horatio outlined the investigative plans.

"After a precursory analysis, my partners at the Head Office feel that there is a link between the disappearance of Claude at this time and the unexplained circumstances affecting the business. In addition to examining the business transactions, we are employing the services of an International Private Investigation firm. We have worked with this firm in the past and can attest to their professionalism and integrity. No one will know of their investigation. Their primary involvement will be to research any possible threats or actions against Claude or the family. You can be assured of their total discretion. My initial concern is whether anything may have arisen as a result of the recent kidnapping of Claude's daughter. While the facts of the Rarotongan family's involvement negated the possibility of any third party being responsible, it has opened up the potential vulnerability for others to attempt blackmail. The unexplained attitude of suppliers and weakened relationships to de Passioné controlled businesses will require some intense investigation."

Barry placed his hands on the table and leaned forward to address Horatio.

"I understand the need for you to examine the finances and to undertake the investigations, but remember, we have a business to keep operational. I'm no bloody accountant or PI. I am an expert in winemaking, and while I will assist you, I need to be involved with the staff and keep things running. I need you and your people to be as unobtrusive as possible. We don't need more rumors started by our people. Do I have your word for this?"

"You do. We will answer any questions that may arise with a statement to the effect that we are working on behalf of an interested business partner who is seeking independent assurance that de Passioné Estates will be able to supply and meet a long-term commitment."

"That will be perfect. No point in stirring up more trouble."

The side door to the dining area opened, and Buzz escorted a more conservatively dressed Marie-France into the room. The guests stood out of respect as she walked to take a seat at the table. Buzz pulled back an antique dining chair for her to join them all at the table. As she sat down, the sound of a loud fart emanated from her. Embarrassed silence immediately fell around the table, followed by laughter. Marie-France nonchalantly exclaimed, "Sacré bleu. Better out than in." The guests watched in disbelief as she then reached for a large plate of flatulent-causing oysters.

The meal resumed. Barry addressed Buzz.

"Buzz, can you spend a few minutes with me alone after ?"

Puzzled, Buzz responded. "Of course."

After the group had finished eating, a cheese plate was offered, then coffee or after-dinner drinks. The guests declined and excused themselves. "Thank you, but we will retire as tomorrow will be a busy day for us."

Marie-France was requested by Buzz to give him and Barry time alone.

Chapter 15

Capovaticano Resort Thalasso Spa, Calabria, Italy

Luigi Fratti's mood was foul. He suspected that Donna Romano, his wife, had been involved in the death of his mistress, Bianca Barbieri.

He glowered at her suspiciously across the hotel's elaborately furnished living room. Bianca had been a strong swimmer and in excellent health. There was no reason for her death in the hotel pool.

Donna sat flipping through the pages of a fashion magazine, pretending to ignore Luigi and his stare.

The silence was broken by Luigi.

"I know you were in some way responsible for her death. Your behavior toward Bianca over the past few months has been despicable. I am surprised she continued working for us."

"Do you think I am that stupid? I have been watching you and the way you carried on around her. You have never explained your long absences during the day, especially those days when you went to the market. I have never believed your excuses for attending business meetings. Those thugs you meet with always come to our home for meetings, and in fact, some have arrived while you are supposedly at meetings where they are meant to be. I said nothing. I expected your affair with her to end when you got bored or a new one took your attention."

Enraged, Luigi flew across the room, his fists raised. As he was about to beat her, a small voice called out.

"Papa, don't hurt Mama. Please don't hit her."

"Maria, go back to bed. Papa is not going to hurt me. We are talking, and he is angry, but he will not harm me. I promise."

As Maria slowly turned to head back to her room, Luigi slumped down into the chair next to Donna.

"Donna, you are in no position to lecture me. I saw Vito Colangelo outside. How did he know we were here? He has no business in this area. Bianca had told me that he had been at the Villa as well. She saw the two of you together more than once. You are still having an affair with that bum. He's a loser. I should send him a message from me that he won't forget."

"You are a fucking hypocrite as well as a low life who fucks our assistants and creates unhappiness wherever you go or what you do. You are scum."

"What did you do to Bianca? Did you poison her? What did you use? Did that Vito help you?"

"I wish I had, and no, I did not kill her, and Vito has morals a lot higher than yours. He would never kill anyone."

Donna thought back to her earlier conversation with Vito and remembered the look on his face when she spotted him near the pool containing Bianca's body. She wondered whether he had reacted based on her complaints to him about Bianca and Luigi.

"I was planning to talk to you about dismissing Bianca. I have been angry at her recently as I have discovered that she has stolen certain items from me. One of my men in the police found out she had been working with a street gang and was attempting to sell my items. She had also betrayed us to the police and told them of certain confidential information she must have snooped on in my office. It is good she is dead,"

Now, Donna wondered whether Luigi or one of his men had killed her. She considered this possibility as well as the possibility of Vito Colangelo having murdered her.

"What had she stolen or told the police?"

Luigi turned and faced her. His look of anger returned.

"I have told you before not to ask or try to get involved in my business. Do you understand?"

"I understand, and now I am going to go and comfort Maria. You scared her with your little temper outburst. Was that just you, or was the cocaine helping?

Luigi jumped to his feet and slapped her with such force that she staggered several feet and fell to the floor. He looked down and spat on her as he walked from the room.

"Bitch."

"If you or your men killed her, the evidence will be discovered by the coroner. You won't get away with this murder," she yelled after him.

Sitting outside in his parked car, Vito watched as ambulance attendants and police swarmed around. He saw Bianca's body being wheeled on a stretcher and placed in the ambulance.

Quietly, he sat and wondered what Donna Romano had used to kill her, as he recalled her earlier fury.

There was a loud knocking on the hotel door. Donna rose and opened the door to find two uniformed police officers.

"Sorry to disturb you. We need to come in and ask you some questions about Bianca Barbieri, your house assistant. As we are sure you know, Miss Barbieri has been found deceased."

"I will call my husband, Luigi, as he hired her and managed the business relationship."

"No, we wish to speak to each of you privately. How long had Miss Barbieri worked for you? Did she live with you and your family, or did she have her own apartment? Did you ever meet any of her friends?"

"Why are you asking me these questions? She simply did errands for us, and besides assisting with maintaining the villa in Calabria, she looked after my daughter Maria. She had her apartment and kept her personal life private."

The two officers exchanged glances and then continued.

"Were you aware that Miss Barbieri had a male friend here whom she was seen with shortly before her body was found? A Vito Colangelo. We believe you know this man."

Donna was shocked. She backed into the room and sat back down in the chair.

"No, I did not know she was friends with him. I did have a relationship with Vito long before I married Luigi, but there was nothing between us anymore. This afternoon, I had a brief conversation with him when he was walking back from the beach. I had no idea he was staying here or that he was involved with Bianca."

"We are going to need you to accompany us to the Carabinieri station for more questioning, but first, we need to speak to your husband. Where is he?"

"He is in his office. You may find he is upset over the death of Bianca. I will call him to join us."

"No, we will go to his office. We wish to speak with him alone."

"Nobody goes to his office. He does not allow anyone access."

"We are the police. We are investigating a possible murder. Either he admits us or we will call a judge and obtain an order or request him to attend here. Take us to his office."

Donna stood and led the officers across to a stairway up to a mezzanine floor. She knocked loudly on the solid mahogany door. There was shouting and cursing from within. Not to be deterred, one of the officers hammered on the door and announced they needed to speak with him on police business. A string of vulgar curses ensued, but the door was opened by a disheveled Luigi who reeked of strong alcohol.

The police turned to Donna. "You may leave us now. Wait downstairs for us."

The two officers entered Luigi's office and loudly closed the door. Once inside, Luigi smiled and shook their hands. "Enzo and Mario, thank God it's you who are here investigating that unfortunate incident with Bianca Barbieri. Here, let me get you both a drink while we talk."

Luigi crossed to his bar and poured two Camparis for the officers. He handed them each a drink and motioned for them to take a seat on the large couch.

"It's been a while since we spoke. If I remember correctly, it was the last 'raid' you were involved in. Pity it was a waste of time for all those officers. I hope the consulting fee you both received for the information was adequate. Now, what can I answer for you?

"We have been given strong evidence of your affair with Bianca Barbieri. Did you kill her or arrange her killing? Tell us so we can 'manage' this investigation."

"No, I did not. My bitch of a wife had found out about our affair and was scheming something. I think she enlisted the assistance of Vito Colangelo, and together they killed her. He was a former lover of hers and was still crazy about her. She hated Bianca. I was going to leave her and live with Bianca. I am angry and want her punished. I am relying on you to help me."

The officer named Enzo smiled before speaking. "Luigi, it is unfortunate, but I have a large unexpected personal expense and will need to take a leave from the Carabinieri for a lengthy period. They will be replacing me with an officer from Solerno. I do not think Mario and I will be able to conclude this case before I leave. I could delay my departure under the right circumstances."

He looked over at Mario, who was resting back on the couch and amused. They both knew of Luigi's past and involvement with the Mafia. An opportunity had just been dropped into their laps.

"I, too, will be taking a vacation leave to take my wife to New York for a month, then traveling to California, so I will be gone. This case will be handled by others."

Luigi quickly realized the situation. "Maybe I can help you both," he said as he walked to his desk and unlocked a drawer. He withdrew a metal box from which he took a large stack of paper money. He placed the money on his desk. "Now, excuse me. I need to use the toilet."

Luigi left the room and after several minutes returned. The cash on the desk was gone.

"Luigi, thank you for the drinks and your cooperation. We must leave now and take Donna with us to the station, as she is a suspect in the murder of Bianca Barbieri."

The two officers smiled and gave Luigi informal salutes as they descended the stairs to arrest Donna.

Luigi smiled as he listened to the howls of protest from Donna as she was forcibly escorted from the hotel room.

There was a click, and the door to his office swung open. Standing in the doorway with her favorite doll nestled in her arms was Maria.

"Papa, papa, who were those men? Where have they taken Mama?"

"Don't worry, they just need to ask her some questions. She will return soon."

Maria stood looking at him with a sad expression on her face.

"Papa, I hate you. You are mean and cruel."

Sobbing, Maria ran from the room. She felt alone and lost.

Chapter 16

Tantamore Capital Finance Group, Canary Wharf, London, UK.

The day started badly for Sir Reginald Coxburn. The typical cold and rainy weather of London's autumn did not help. He had overslept after his night of debauchery with several of London's ladies of the night. At his age, the excessive drinking, drugs, and sex had taken their toll.

Sir Reginald scraped himself out of the strange bed of some whore, whose name he could not remember. He found himself alone in a small flat. Upon checking his clothes, he found his wallet with his credit cards and personal papers missing. He cursed.

He pulled on yesterday's clothes and climbed down the dingy stairway to hail a taxi to take him to his office. Outside, the wind lashed the cold freezing rain against his face. The driving rain soon soaked through his expensive Saville Row suit, and the overflowing rain from the gutter saturated his expensive hand-crafted Barker shoes.

He waved for a taxi. A typical black London taxi pulled toward him and, in the process, splashed more water on him. Sir Reginald cursed and complained to the driver, which only drew a cockney response laced with profanities. Sir Reginald wondered what had happened to manners and civility. It seemed no one respected distinguished gentlemen anymore.

Even with the council's attempt to regulate traffic in London's business district, there was still massive congestion. Sir Reginald looked at his watch and cursed. He would be late for his teleconference with Arnie Jacobson, and his parasitic crew who passed themselves off as investment brokers. In frustration, he shouted to the driver to find another way to his office.

"Guv, There ain't no other bloody way at this time of day, so I suggest you shut your hole, sit back, and enjoy the ride."

The rain had intensified. Visibility through the windows was nonexistent. Sir Reginald's fury increased. He hated that he would allow Arnie Jacobson to take the upper hand due to his lateness. He could tell what type of day he was facing.

Just as the traffic started to move, there was an intense jolt, and the old taxi jerked forward and collided with the curb. They had been rear-ended. The driver was furious and jumped out of his seat into the beating and blowing rain. Within minutes, fists were flying between the driver and the man who had hit them. Sir Reginald decided he would probably make faster progress by walking, and besides, since his wallet had been stolen, he had no money to pay the irate taxi driver. He quietly opened the passenger door, slipped out into the traffic, and merged amongst the wet and huddled pedestrians fighting the storm on their way to work. Amongst them, he was invisible. Just another wet, cold, and miserable office worker slaving to pay the rent and a few luxuries.

At Canary Wharf, he acknowledged the security guards and continued on his way to the elevator bank. He was soaked, and water was pooling on the tiled floor while he waited for the elevator. Several women waiting for the elevator cast sympathetic looks at him. He was in no mood to respond.

Sir Reginald rode the elevator to the floor where his office was located. He swung open the floor-to-ceiling smoked glass door and strode in. Cindy, the young receptionist, looked up and was about to welcome him before she saw the scowl on his face.

"Call my fucking tailor at Lords and tell him to get his arse over here with a replacement suit and shoes. Tell him to make it quick. And good day to you."

He stormed off to his office and left strict instructions not to be disturbed. In his office, he stripped naked and plunged into his private shower. He stood under the luxurious stream of hot water and soaked away the remnants of last night and the events of the morning. He emerged from the shower and dressed in a thick terry robe, which would suffice until his tailor arrived with replacement clothing.

He checked the time. He still had 15 minutes until the scheduled teleconference with Arnie Jacobson.

"Cindy," he called. "Did you reach Lords? Did they tell you when they can deliver a set of replacement clothing for me?"

"They promised to bring a set here in approximately 30 minutes."

"Good, now contact Arnie Jacobson's office in New York. Advise them that due to a weather delay and problems here, our call is delayed by an hour."

"Yes, sir."

Sir Reginald had barely finished speaking, and Cindy was dialing the number.

Sir Reginald felt his mood lightening. It improved when Dolores, his matronly office manager, arrived with a tray containing a freshly brewed pot of tea and fresh cream buns. Dolores always knew how to tame the emotions of Sir Reginald.

Cindy confirmed the new time for the delayed teleconference. He was pleased and decided to obtain an update from his traders located on the floor below. He walked over to the internal stairway that linked the two office floors and emerged into a downstairs area populated with computer screens and young employees shouting to each other about the changing conditions of the market.

Sir Reginald loved the noise and vitality of the Trading floor. He was curious to see a small group clustered around the desk of the trader who handled private funds.

"What is happening? Why is everyone gathered here? Is there something major happening?"

Upon his arrival at the desk, several of the employees looked at him apprehensively and then retreated to their respective desks, leaving Charles Windsor, the private funds' investment manager, to explain.

Charles Windsor bent forward and tapped the keys of his terminal. Sir Reginald looked up at the screen. A green line spiraled down to a yellow line that divided the screen into two parts. The green line continued down but had changed to red. Toward the bottom of the screen, a large black X stopped the line. The word HALT was superimposed over the X.

"Charles, what the hell is that? What is happening?"

"Sir, the funds you directed invested from the Arnie Jacobson hedge fund were sold short today in New York. The investment has lost all value, and the residual value of the investment has collapsed. It is a disaster. We are going to take an enormous loss."

"Which companies were affected? Who has sustained the largest loss?"

"Sir, you had emphatically insisted on our taking a major position in de Passioné Estates and their Mondial company. The investment is now worthless, and de Passioné had distributed the funds in different working capital pools for their investments in the different operations. Unless the investment banks for de Passioné come to the rescue, that company is finished."

"Charles, what and who started this slide?"

"The transaction history shows an overnight series of trades and selling associated with Arnie Jacobson Hedge Funds."

"That slimey son of a bitch. Let me at him."

Sir Reginald stormed off to face the unpleasantness of the teleconference call with Arnie and his minions.

Chapter 17

de Passioné Estates, France

Pandemonium reigned in the offices of de Passioné Estates. Phones were constantly ringing, and several courier firms had arrived with urgent mail. The time difference between North America and France allowed parties with interests in de Passioné Estates to react. Major wholesale distribution agreement cancellations were received, citing the company's insolvency and alluding to the now-known operational problems.

Barry Jones was overwhelmed. Buzz participated in reviewing the incoming assault of legal documents and correspondence. Horatio Henderson and Sylvia Piper enlisted the support of other lawyers in their head office.

Mid-afternoon, Barry took a call he had hoped would never come. The director of PariVest Industrial and Commercial Bank in Paris was calling. Other senior managers from different investment banks in Germany, Switzerland, Austria, and several leading analysts for the major brokerages were on the call to participate.

The situation was dire. The banks were insisting on speaking to Claude. All of the participants were seeking confirmation that the family's private funds would be deployed to prevent a complete crash of the company. Without Claude's presence and control, no such assurance could be given.

Horatio Henderson took control.

"Gentlemen, there is no need for panic. We are in the process of unraveling who and what is behind these sudden, unwarranted events. It seems at this stage there is no foundation for any of the actions that have occurred. In our early investigations, we have identified actions that were deliberately taken by individuals to cripple the operations of de Passioné Estates. These actions were criminal, and we will be pursuing whatever legal recourse is possible. The companies are in excellent operating condition, and these efforts to create upheaval in the company are unfounded. The companies are solid. We need some time to investigate further and request your patience. The investigations will be transparent, and all information we uncover will be shared."

Questions and comments were passed between the participants on the call. One final question, however, could not be answered.

Where was Claude de Passioné, and did he know about these events? Was he hiding due to this? Was Marie-France able to act for the family companies?

Barry took control and assured them that soon Claude would be able to address their concerns.

Unhappily, the participants grumbled and agreed to delay any precipitous actions and wait to hear from Claude.

With the call finished, Barry, Buzz, Horatio, and Sylvia sat looking at each other, not sure how to proceed. Buzz decided to take control.

"As some of you here are aware, I served in various roles for the US Government that had me in deep contact with the FBI, CIA, and other intelligence agencies. During my career, I operated overseas and with some individuals who now occupy some senior positions. Based on that conference call, we must locate Claude and get him back here without delay. I am going to leave France as soon as I can arrange things and enlist the support of those individuals."

Horatio sat and stared at Buzz. He steepled his fingers together and pursed them to his lips. Finally, he spoke.

"Ordinarily, I would counsel against getting any of those government organizations involved. There is no way of assuring that sensitive information will not be leaked to the wrong parties, but given the severity of the situation here, there is nothing to lose."

Barry, who had been listening to an interchange between Buzz and Horatio, interrupted.

"I suggest we split the situation into two categories. One is the need to find Claude, and the second is to investigate the sabotage of the businesses. Rather than use our resources trying to pursue both issues combined, we should divide into teams, each with a specific mission."

Horatio and Buzz nodded their approval. Buzz turned to Barry and spoke.

"Barry, I have a suggestion. We know that Claude took that flight from Rarotonga to Tahiti in the morning. We know he checked into the hotel and after that disappeared. You and Yvette had met and spent time with Denis Ricard, the French Cultural Attache. The French Polynesian Islands are administered through his office in San Francisco. I suggest you establish contact with him and enlist his support. He has access to information in Tahiti that we would otherwise struggle to get from the French bureaucracy. I am sure Denis could assist. If we can get him to investigate any known criminal presence there, that would be helpful. I can work with my sources and investigate any individuals he exposes."

For the next hour, they sat and discussed different strategies, and a plan was agreed upon. Barry would fly to Tahiti, Buzz would fly to the US, and Horatio and staff from his firm would temporarily assume management of the business.

Barry was the first to leave. He went to the quiet of his room and placed the first of the calls he needed to make. His first call was to the French Consulate in San Francisco. The phone was answered by the same receptionist with whom Barry had previously clashed. She recognized Barry's thick Australian accent. Her cold Parisian attitude dripped through the phone.

Within minutes, Denis Ricard, the French Cultural Attache, answered.

"Bonjour, I am pleased to hear from you. I have been following the news regarding the de Passioné businesses. What has gone wrong?"

"Denis, I will be coming to San Francisco. I need to fly to Tahiti and need your assistance. Can we meet?"

"Of course, but when are you flying to Tahiti? I will be traveling there in the next day or so on business."

Barry was relieved. Traveling with Denis would break the monotony of the flight, plus give him time to brief Denis on the situation with Claude in Tahiti.

"Denis, let me know your flight arrangements, and I will adjust my schedule."

"Better still, Barry, I will have the flights booked by our staff here. The earliest I can leave is two days from now."

"Denis, that will be great. I will plan to meet you at the airport."

"Barry, I must inform you that from an official position, there will be very little I can offer to assist in helping with the affairs of Claude and de Passioné Estates. The company and its founders have a long history in France. The French Government is reluctant to get involved. There are now some large multinational companies that are headquartered outside of France or French territories that have expressed interest in investing. The government does not want to be seen or promote any actions that will be seen as adverse to foreign investment in French business. There is too much at stake. The government has been handling insurrections by the farmers regarding restrictions and protection of markets that they feel are being eroded in favor of foreign competition. This has impacted the government's attempts to attract foreign investment into the auto industry, pharmaceuticals, and food. If the government takes a position of protecting de Passioné, it could be used as propaganda to claim protectionism. Unofficially, I will assist to the extent I can."

Barry listened quietly and did not respond. He realized his quest to locate Claude using official resources was going to be limited, both in France and Tahiti. In his mind, he resolved to find and expose the inherent dark forces of the corporate manipulation that was occurring.

"Denis, I understand, but I hope that any information you can provide me to find Claude, you will share."

"Of course, my friend. Now I must go and attend to the planning of tonight's function. I will have my office call you with travel arrangements and see you at the airport tomorrow."

Barry realized he had been dismissed.

Chapter 18

Intercontinental Hotel and Resort, Tahiti

Vicky returned from the bathroom to find Claude somewhat alert, sitting and staring out of the massive glass window that overlooked the beach and coast.

She stood close to his side and handed him the glass of wine containing the liquid Viagra. Claude took the wine and wrapped his fumbling fingers around the glass. He looked up at Vicky and smiled a charming smile. She returned the smile and recalled why they called her 'The Vixen'. She would seduce and render Claude helpless.

It was obvious to Vicky that the earlier flirtations of the afternoon were not wasted. Claude seemed to retain the desires that were overriding the impact of the drugs. Vicky was flattered that he was able to focus on her even in his state. She wondered what impact the Viagra would have.

She did not have long to wait for the answer.

"Vicky, I believe a walk along the beach will help me. I have been feeling drowsy and lethargic and need to go out and enjoy the fresh air of the evening."

A mild panic set in. Vicky did not want to be seen with Claude by any of the patrons at the hotel. Especially certain guests.

"Claude, that is a fantastic idea. I will shower and change into something more appropriate. I suggest you do the same.

Vicky trailed her hand over Claude's shoulder and left for the bathroom. She emerged minutes later and proceeded to her bedroom to change. Claude slowly rose and went to the shower.

As he walked to the bathroom, Claude experienced an erection and feelings he had not known since his youth. Though still feeling groggy, he smiled as he recalled certain of his youthful paramours. It seemed to him that the time he was spending in Tahiti and with Vicky was healing his mood of loss and dejection. The tempestuous collapse of his marriage and the loss of his ideal life in Rarotonga had borne heavily on him.

He brushed away the immediate memories of his life in Rarotonga with Atarangi, his beautiful Island wife, as his feelings for Vicky grew.

Claude stripped his clothes and soaked under the steady stream of warm water that cascaded down from the rainshower head. The warm water intensified Claude's mental desire for Vicky, and the arousal he experienced grew. Again, Claude thought back to his youth. He did not understand the present situation. He looked down at his erect enlarged penis and wondered why it was happening. There was no one present to excite him.

Claude ended the shower and stepped out to dress casually for the beach walk. He was confused. His erection was larger, and his desire for Vicky was increasing. He turned his thoughts away from her and focused on the family's wine business. It was a useless exercise as the thoughts and desires returned immediately.

Vicky was standing in the living area dressed in a loose, long white dress. She wore brown open-toed sandals and was adorned with a simple gold necklace. Claude was amazed at the transformation from the hard, business-like woman's appearance to the image that now stood in front of him. The dark, drab business clothing was gone. The harsh makeup and tight hair had been replaced with those yielding a softer look.

"Come, Claude. Let's make our way down to the beach. I want to avoid the crowded lobby and the noise of all those people. We will go down through the bar and out the open exit past the pool and onto the beach."

Claude agreed. After all he had experienced over the last month, he preferred avoiding any crowd.

"Yes, I agree. We will blend in discreetly with the tourists at the bar, but will not stop."

Vicky was happy that he agreed. She did not want anyone paying too much attention to them.

She looked at how he was dressed. In his casual chinos, flip-flops, and pale T-shirt, he passed as any of the nondescript male tourists at the hotel.

They left the room and strolled arm-in-arm along the corridor and through the busy bar, like a honeymoon couple. The number of people at the pool was thinning out as many had left to freshen up for early cocktails or dinner.

Small groups stood together on the beach waiting to see and photograph the magnificent sunset that the hotel was renowned for. Waiters scurried around the groups, plying them with cocktails and eager for generous tips.

Pretending to be a couple deeply in love, Vicky and Claude continued to stroll arm-in-arm along the beach at the water's edge. Small waves splashed up onto the sand. Claude dropped to his knees and removed Vicky's sandals and then his own, before

playfully pulling her into the water to walk with him. She offered
no resistance.

Wrapped up in the atmosphere of the hotel and beach, Vicky had
inadvertently let her guard down. She was oblivious to the
presence of the tail, which was stalking them from a distance.

Sir Reginald Coxburn had cunningly foreseen the action that Arnie
Jacobson had planned. Furthermore, he distrusted Luigi Fratti and
the others involved in the scheme to capture the de Passioné family
businesses. Sir Reginald had not achieved his position in life by
being gullible and accepting deals and agreements as they were
presented to them. He possessed the senses of a cunning fox.

Unsettled by recent events and his growing distrust, he had
deployed his trusted enforcer, Knuckles O'Brien, to monitor Vicky
and, if required to deal with her and Claude in whatever manner
was needed.

Knuckles stayed a discreet distance behind and followed Vicky and
Claude as they walked the beach. He was dressed as a typical
uneducated tourist, complete with an SLR camera hung around his
neck, Roman sandals, and knee-high white socks, and wearing a
garish bright pink shirt of hibiscus flowers.

His appearance ensured that most of the other tourists steered away
from the eccentric and slightly deranged Irishman. Women would
automatically need to attend to a matter if they saw Knuckles
approaching. His disguise was perfect for the job.

From time to time, Knuckles would stop and stare out at the ocean
while holding the camera and pretending to capture the setting sun.
To the casual observer, he was just another lonely, unattached
bachelor tourist enjoying a well-deserved trip to Tahiti.

Knuckles watched as Vicky and Claude reached the deserted end of the beach and entered a cave eroded into the low cliff by years of the ocean pounding the rock base.

Inside the cave, the setting sun's rays reflected on the ragged rock walls, creating a mystic feel. This only served to increase Claude's erotic and romantic mood. He reached for Vicky and pulled her toward him, but she pushed him away with her hands against his chest.

"Claude, you must remember that you are not free to do as you wish. Others are looking for you. It is my responsibility to guard you and ensure your safety until we can take you to our secure location."

"I am unsure what it is you are talking about. I am Claude de Passioné, head of the de Passioné family businesses. I have only recently separated from my wife in Rarotonga and am taking a small vacation before returning to France and the business. What do you mean others are looking for me? Who are you?"

"I am a special security agent. I told you I work for Tantamore Capital. I have been sent here to protect you by investors who are concerned for your safety. If you check the recent business pages, you will read that de Passioné businesses are under a lot of external pressure, which is affecting the operations of the companies. It is believed you are in danger from certain parties," she lied.

Claude was dumbfounded. He stared at her in disbelief.

"But, I don't understand. I spoke to Barry Jones, my trusted executive in charge, only a few days ago. He informed me all is well. That was on Wednesday. What day is it today?"

"It is Tuesday. You slept for days after arriving here. I was worried and considered calling for medical help."

"We must go back to the hotel immediately. I must contact Barry or others in my office. This is serious. Let's go"

Claude rushed toward the entrance but was blocked by Vicky.

"Be careful, Claude. Let me check outside first."

Vicky crawled from the cave. She scanned the beach and was startled to see the silhouette of Knuckles O'Brien standing and looking directly at the entrance to the cave.

"Claude, we will need to stay in here. There is a man out there I know. He is a gangster. I have had dealings with him in the past. He is dangerous. I am not sure whether he is looking for me or you. We must be careful and leave the hotel as soon as possible. It is no longer safe for you to be there."

Claude leaned against the rock wall and tried to understand the events that had occurred since he left Rarotonga. The drugs had distorted his memory. His recollection of days and happenings was a blur. It seemed the major thought that continually recurred was his unexplainable attraction to Vicky, though he had never met or known her before. He was fixated on her. Feeling mentally confused, Claude slowly joined her at the cave entrance, where she stood watching Knuckles O'Brien.

Chapter 19

Tantamore Capital, London, UK

Sir Reginald's mood continued to be as stormy as the predictable British weather. His night had not gone well. His anger swelled at the thought that Arnie Jacobs had attempted to usurp his control and power in the massive grab to seize ownership and control of the de Passioné interests.

Sir Reginald looked out at the early grey dawn sky over London. It was a time of day he hated, and the swirling, misty light rain did nothing to alleviate his feelings.

It was too early for any of the administrative staff to arrive, so Sir Reginald decided to visit the floor below, where the traders had spent the night working the exchanges in Asia and America, and where he knew he could find some good coffee.

As he entered the trading floor, the senior trader approached him.

"Sir, there have been some developments affecting de Passioné and our holdings. There has been a flurry of unexplained activity from Australia and Hong Kong. We are attempting to obtain more information. The exchanges in America have issued a trading halt. Something big is happening."

This was not the news that Sir Reginald needed to start his day.

"Make it a priority. Get your best people on it. I want a report and review as soon as possible. I will be waiting."

Sir Reginald poured a coffee and climbed the stairs back up to his office. As he sat wondering who was behind these recent events, he was interrupted by the shrill whistle from his secure private phone. He looked at it and tried to determine who would call him at such an early hour. He reached for the phone.

He barely had the phone raised to his ear when the verbal assault began.

"Vicky, my dear. Calm down. What has upset my special Vixen? You are in a paradise doing a simple job."

His comment only served to infuriate her more.

"You son of a bitch. Why the fuck have you sent Knuckles."

Before she finished, he hung up the phone. With his mood, the disclosure of news regarding de Passioné, and the gloomy weather, he was in no mood to put up with her. He was further infuriated to know that Knuckles O'Brien's presence had been discovered. He had wanted Knuckles to track her, without her knowledge, as he did not fully trust her. His past experiences with her made him suspicious.

He considered with anger the considerable expenses of sending Knuckles to Tahiti. A £7500 airfare, a $1200US a night hotel room, daily expenses, and then Knuckles' daily 'consulting' rate.

While fuming, his private phone rang again.

"OK, Vixen. Have you calmed down? I also suggest you find some respect for me. You are in no position to demand or threaten me. I have too much on you to have the authorities put you away for a long time. Worse, some of our associates could engineer an early demise for you and your plans."

"Why did you send him? This is a plan I brought to you. I am not about to do anything to jeopardize it. I have our prize safely guarded here away from any interference."

"Vixen, my dear, let's just call it past experiences, shall we?"

"Shall we say that my experiences with you have shown you to be a real slimy bastard? You are no one to talk about trust."

"It is for your safety. There have been some developments you are unaware of."

Sir Reginald spent the next while updating her on the actions of Arnie Jacobson and the reports he had received from Italy. He edited the information he shared to slant it in his favor. In the end, Vicky seemed calm but still did not trust him.

After the call, Vicky checked the time. It was 8:30 pm. She had waited to call Sir Reginald, recognizing the 10-hour time difference. Feeling calmer after the call and concerned about the impact of the drugs and the Viagra on Claude, she decided to wake him from his slumber and visit the hotel restaurant, but first, she decided to check for the presence of Knuckles O'Brien.

As she was about to leave the room, her phone rang. She looked at the screen. It was Sir Reginald calling.

"What now? Do you miss me?"

"Vicky, it is important for you to get Claude hidden. It seems that some of his people are traveling to Tahiti in search of him. You need to be very careful. My people here are trying to determine the sources of the financial activities in Australia and China. Events are happening that we never foresaw. I can understand some interest from Australian financial groups who are invested in the Australian wine industry, but China is inexplicable. Be aware of any Oriental presence who may be watching you or displaying interest. Something is wrong."

"Thank you, Reggie. I will immediately take action."

Sir Reginald hung up and sat trying to piece together the players and the motives. A loud knock on his office door preceded the entry of his receptionist, followed by a well-dressed middle-aged man. Sir Reginald immediately recognized him.

"Lord Thornberry. What a pleasure. What brings you to London, especially on a day like today with such inclement weather?"

"Oh, dear man. A little rain won't hurt. We faced much worse than this during that damned Falklands War. I was sure my vessel was incapable of withstanding the pounding of those seas and the howling gales. What a godforsaken part of the world. Cold, barren, and hostile. We should have let them keep it."

"To what do I owe the pleasure of your company, Lord?"

"It seems some influential members of a certain family have interests in France. In particular, those interests are currently experiencing some turmoil. Naturally, the family would like anonymity and to withdraw their interests without loss."

"That may not be possible. In New York, they have suspended all trading pending an announcement. I will consult with the head trader, and if there is a favorable development, we will, with total discretion, undertake steps to recover their interests and protect the confidentiality of their involvement."

"Excellent, then. Good man. I knew we could trust you. You must come to the club one day for a fox hunt. Until then, goodbye. My secretary will contact you to arrange for you to visit."

Sir Reginald stood and shook hands with Lord Thornberry.

"It's been a while since we spoke. Good of you to invite me. I look forward to it."

While being outwardly courteous, Sir Reginald despised Lord Thornberry and patiently awaited his departure. He was eager to contact Arnie Jacobson.

He settled back behind his desk and checked the time. It was late afternoon in New York. The Stock Exchange would now have ceased the day's trading. Sir Reginald considered it an ideal time to speak with Arnie Jacobson.

Jacobson's personal phone was answered on the first ring.

"Sir Reginald. I was wondering when you would call. I assume you are calling to get more information on the de Passioné situation. There are not a lot of facts known yet. It appears there is a friendly white knight who is prepared to invest and restructure the business. The identities of these people are being closely guarded, though many rumors and guesses are circulating here. What's the situation there in London? Any accurate information?"

"None that I know of. There is one piece of information circulating here that I do not understand. According to our sources, there is Chinese involvement. Do you know anything about this?"

"That is interesting, as we are hearing that as well. I am suspicious, as the rumor has been shared with us by several of our sources. If it is true, and supposedly, if the deal is meant to be confidential, then why has it been leaked to different brokerages? I guess that it is a deliberate leak from the Chinese government. What I do not understand is what China stands to gain from owning a major wine and liquor company. This is a strange diversion from their normal interest and acquisitions of industrial companies."

Sir Reginald considered the information Arnie had shared.

"By acquiring de Passioné, they end up with a label that is only marginally beaten out of first place by a certain family-owned rum company. But you are correct. It is a departure from the norm for them."

"There has to be another reason, Reggie, and we don't see it yet. Anyway, any attempt to muscle in will be met with strong opposition. We will provide more funding to take the de Passioné businesses. Is Tantamore good for the capital to mount a fight?"

"Trust me, Arnie, more than capable. That won't be necessary."

Chapter 20

Calabria, Italy

Luigi Fratti was pleased to be back home at his villa. His 'vacation' had not gone well. His mistress, Bianca Barbieri, was dead. The circumstances of her death were suspicious. He suspected his wife, Donna Romano, had been involved. They had argued about Bianca. Earlier, he had seen her previous lover lurking in the bushes near the pool in which she had died. The questioning of his wife by the local police was inconclusive. He decided it was time for Donna to disappear from his life, especially with the scheme he had agreed to participate in with The Vixen. He needed no distractions; besides, he was bored with her. Even though she was amazingly beautiful, she was annoying him and asking too many questions about his business. He wondered whether he should demand custody over Maria, their daughter, or let her go with Donna. He decided to send her with Donna. He did not need a prying daughter interfering with his plans.

As he sat thinking about his situation, the phone on his desk jangled, startling him. He reached and picked up the receiver.

"Pronto"

He waited until a hoarse and whispering voice spoke.

"We have a little problem with the package in Tahiti. Seems the storage area is no longer safe. We need to arrange a new warehouse."

Luigi cursed. He had considered the Intercontinental Hotel as the most secure location in which Vicky could keep Claude away from detection. He considered the options and decided it was time to contact Vicky directly.

"Thank you for the information. I will contact the warehouse manager and have our packages moved to a secure location."

The phone call clicked dead as the mysterious caller disconnected.

Luigi sat digesting the information and deciding on a course of action. He looked at his watch. With the 11-hour time difference between Calabria and Tahiti, it made no sense to call Vicky in the middle of the night.

After some thought, Luigi decided to call Sir Reginald Coxburn. He was the one whom Vicky had convinced to structure the scheme to seize control of the de Passioné businesses. He had better control over Vicky. He reached for the phone and punched in the numbers for Sir Reginald's private and secure sat phone.

"Good evening, Reggie. It appears there is a problem with our shipment. It seems some others are interested and could cause some interference with the shipment."

"Do you have any details? I have one of my trusted men there. Do I need to contact him to make arrangements?"

"No. I mentioned to you earlier that Tahiti is too small for things to go undetected. If you still wish to proceed and want our investment, I suggest you get the package to me in Italy."

"I doubt that is possible. The only way off that island is by air, and you can be sure the airport is closely monitored."

"I suggest you use your imagination and send in a private plane. We can arrange some local assistance to get the package on the plane undetected."

Luigi sensed his frustration growing with the Englishman. He wondered at the ability of Reggie to handle the transactions required to manipulate the financial collapse of the de Passioné family businesses. He wished Vicky had confided in him and avoided Sir Reginald's involvement. It was too late now. He listened as the conversation droned on.

"Luigi, I suggest we arrange a plan before I contact The Vixen and my man there. I don't want them stirring things up. If you have contacts, it might be better to use them."

"I do, but it will cost to get things organized, and it will take some time. Are the goods in Tahiti secure? Is the situation under control?"

"I have full confidence in The Vixen. I do not anticipate any problems in that regard."

"I hope not for your sake. The consequences of failure for this project are huge and involve others beyond my control. See to it that things there are stable."

Sir Reginald grimaced at the threat. Nobody spoke to him in that manner. Deep down, he had no time for the Italian mobster, and had it not been for Vicky's insistence, he would not have included him. He was aware of some of the other players and wondered what their relationships with Luigi were like. He decided it was time to test the water and find out.

"Luigi, you need not worry about my abilities, but since there are others involved, I will contact the New York party. He must be advised of this development."

"No fucking way. This is between us. I do not want or trust others to know of the logistics for the storage and shipping of our merchandise. Do you understand?"

"Luigi, the costs to execute the project are huge and require the assistance of New York. They need to be intimately involved in each step. I speak from experience. In many ways, they are more ruthless than your men."

"That is a matter of opinion, and I strongly suggest you do not try to find out. Now go and deal with The Vixen. Good night. Let me know when it is done."

Reggie hung up and realized he was being manipulated. He did not like it and decided to contact Arnie Jacobson, not caring that it was the middle of the night. He dialed the number for Arnie's cellphone. He must tell Arnie that the existence of Claude on the island had become known, and the need to get the 'package' off the island.

 A groggy voice answered.

"Who the fuck is calling at this hour? Some drunk? Better be good."

"Arnie, it's Reggie. Call me back on a secure line. We need to talk."

After listening to Reggie, Luigi searched through his list of contacts to find a trusted one in Tahiti. There were none. He would need to send someone to the island. He considered his options before deciding on Antonio (Grease) Bruno, his cousin in Hawaii. He had worked with Antonio when he had lived in Italy, before fleeing to Hawaii to escape the wrath of other gangs. Antonio was discreet and smart.

Luigi walked from his desk to the bar behind the conference table. He poured a vintage Chianti and sat at the table, enjoying the wine while strategizing his next moves while waiting to call Antonio.

He recalled that Vicky had attempted to arrange a trip to Italy with Sir Reginald some months earlier. At the time, he recognized that she was manipulating Sir Reggie and had made excuses to avoid meeting him. His thoughts drifted to the past and the intimate fun he had enjoyed with Vicky. Back then, he had no doubts that she would achieve her own notoriety. Now it was happening.

Chapter 21

de Passioné Residence, France

Barry Jones was tired. It had been a long and exhausting day. He had hastily met with the senior management to delegate control while he was away from the business, searching for Claude. The managers were advised to consult with the lawyer, Horatio Henderson, on all matters should problems arise. Any press or business reporters were to be directed to their PR firm in San Francisco.

As he picked up the few papers he had scattered while organizing his departure from the business, he was startled by the entrance of Marie-France. Unlike her normal eclectic dress, she was wearing a conservative skirt and blouse. She slowly entered the room, all the time keeping her eye fixed on Barry.

"Tell me, Barry. Do you have a hidden secret? Do you know where Claude has gone? I spoke with Buzz, and it seems that Claude's disappearance has some sinister attributes. Surely you must know. He confided in you. Is there another woman involved? Are you and Claude playing some games? Is it about money? We have plenty of money, so there is no need. Tell me, please. Claude is my son. I cannot bear to believe something bad has happened to him."

"Marie-France, I am as concerned as you. No, I have no idea what has happened or why certain things are occurring that are affecting the business. I am going to travel to Tahiti to track his last movements and find out more. It is unlike him, as he always shared most of his personal issues with me."

"When will you leave?"

"I will fly to San Francisco tomorrow and meet with Denis Ricard, the French Cultural Attache in San Francisco. Claude and I had spent time with Denis previously, plus he visited our vineyards here. He has the responsibility for certain matters in Tahiti, and I am hoping he can assist."

"I am worried. Claude is a grown man and has survived some terrible things in the past, but as a mother, I feel he is suffering too much as a result of his marriage collapse and the events that took place in Rarotonga. While he is experienced, I know he has a certain weakness when it comes to romance and emotions."

Barry considered her comment before asking.

"Do you think he would do anything stupid? Could his emotions be so torn apart whereby he may react without thinking?

"I had wondered that, but he has been through so much in his life and never wavered. I suspect he has decided to be alone and has isolated himself from everyone."

"I am not sure I believe that. Claude has never gone incommunicado. You are correct, he has faced some pretty nasty issues in the past. He has dealt with the loss of his fiancée, the day he planned to propose to her. That death shook him immensely. Then there was that terrible situation with the Chinese gangs in San Francisco. He certainly was able to weather those storms. While the collapse of his marriage to Atarangi will affect him, I don't see it being the reason to cease communicating and letting us know what's happening. Not like him at all. I suspect there is more to it."

"My boy always had a fragility about him when it came to women and his affairs. I have faith that between your efforts and those of my stalwart, Buzz, you both will find him, and all will be fine."

"Marie-France, I am not so sure. I will not bother you with all the details, but forces are working against the de Passioné business interests. I have engaged the best people from our law firm, and they are investigating the matter. I request you to remain calm and not venture too far or get into any interactions with parties you do not know. We need to remain focused at this time and do not need any distractions. Your only son is missing, and the de Passioné holdings are under attack. Some of the most prominent bankers in Europe are shaken by the rumors and actions of our vendors with whom we have had excellent long-standing relationships."

"Barry, you insult me. I am a lady of wealth, stature, and intelligence. Because you are unable to control things, doesn't mean I need to stop living."

"Marie-France, let me assure you I am more than capable of controlling matters, but the issues need to be understood."

"You need not worry. My cousin Lady Lydia Agnes Thwacker and her male friend Sir Reginald Coxburn will be visiting here next week. Maybe you should consult with Sir Reginald. He is very successful in business and finance. I am sure he could be of great help."

"Absolutely not. We need to control this and keep the number involved to a minimum. Do not even discuss this with him. It will only lead to more trouble. His reputation isn't as clean as I suspect you think. Now I must leave as I have things to do before my trip."

Marie-France was stunned by Barry's sharp words and reacted.

" You barbaric, uncouth Australian. Why don't you pack up and go back to that backward country? Go have an affair with a kangaroo."

Barry smiled as he walked from the room. As he was exiting, Buzz was walking in.

"Bloody hell, mate. She's primed for takeoff. She's all yours. As you know, I am flying out to San Francisco and then Tahiti. I need you to keep her under control. The whole situation with Claude and the family businesses is fragile, I don't need her to cause any more problems for us. She has those interfering Brits, Lady Lydia and her no-good friend Sir Reginald Coxburn, arriving next week. Try and keep his nose out of our business."

"Shit. It is the worst possible time for them to come. I wonder if I can find a way to delay them."

"Excellent thinking, Buzz. I don't want that Reginald poking around in business that doesn't bloody involve him. Last time he was here I found the cheeky bugger asking the workers questions that should have been of no interest to him. He was digging into our financials and asking about certain people. It was almost like he was spying on us. I couldn't understand it then, but with what is happening now, I wonder if he hasn't got his hand in the goings-on. I don't trust him at all. He has been named in several particularly shady deals over the past couple of years. Seems he is somehow collaborating with a New York sleaze financier called Arnie Jacobson. The FBI has been eager to investigate and charge him. Seems his high-priced attorneys have created enough clouds to obscure matters."

"I hear what you are saying. I still have a lot of contacts from my days with the FBI, so I think I will make a few calls and buy a few rounds of drinks. Do a little off-the-record digging. We need to see what those two have been up to and if there have been any investor research reports issued by Jacobson's firm regarding any of the de Passioné family businesses. When is Sir Reginald due to arrive?"

"He and that Waltzing Matilda, Lydia, are due here next Tuesday. I will be in Tahiti then. I am relying on you to curtail their activities while here."

"That will be my pleasure. How long are they planning on staying?"

"From what Marie-France said, it seems it will be several weeks."

"In that case, I will devise some event that may have them scurrying back the Jolly Old England sooner than they planned. Don't worry, Barry. I had plenty of experience in situations like this."

Barry grinned and shook his head.

"I am sure you do, Buzz. I can only imagine the delights you will plan for them."

Chapter 22

Tahiti Noveau Hotel and Resort, Papette, Tahiti.

After discovering they were being monitored by 'Knuckles' O'Brien, Vicky decided to move back from Bora Bora. The sparse number of guests at the Intercontinental Hotel and too few locals made their presence too obvious. Under her persuasion, they decided to move to the Tahiti Noveau in Papeete. Vicky made up a convincing story about fellow investment bankers who were about to visit and stay in Papeete. Reluctantly, Claude agreed to accompany her. It would be a change, and in truth, he was becoming bored with Bora Bora.

Vicky had deliberately allowed several days to slip by since her explosive call with Sir Reginald. She avoided the calls from Sir Reginald and Luigi. They had annoyed her. There were several messages left by Luigi's hoodlums at the front desk, but she was not intimidated. To make the project work, they all needed her and the secret she possessed.

Holding a glass of the finest chilled white wine, she looked around the room with its soft lighting, complemented by the late afternoon setting sun and dusk. Claude lay sleeping on the couch. It had been a day of relaxation. They had both swum and bathed on the beach under the cloudless bright blue sky. It was as if they were a romantic couple sharing a vacation. Vicky considered it a perfect disguise.

Her eyes fell on the curled body of Claude. Since she had manipulated him, he had said little. She was aware of some of the

Rarotonga events but longed to know more. She found herself becoming more interested in Claude than in the de Passioné business. For years, she had assembled information to plan the financial collapse. All had been proceeding well until Sir Reginald brought in Arnie Jacobson. Things changed then. Within days of Arnie's involvement, the Italian influence was evident, and then the involvement of a powerful Chinese gang.

Vicky opened the sliding doors out to the patio overlooking the ocean. She sat watching the golden sun's last rays as it sank below the horizon while thinking of how her simple plan had morphed into a multinational crime. She wondered if the plan would still work. As the gentle breeze of the ocean caressed her, she relaxed and dozed off into a light sleep.

Claude laid his hand gently on her shoulder. He shook her awake. It was dusk, and reflections of the first lights from the restaurants along the ocean promenade sparkled in the quiet waters of the bay.

She stretched lazily and looked out at the scene. It seemed so far away and unrelated to the current situation she had caused.

To her side, Claude stood quietly observing the panoramic view. Vicky ran her eyes over him. With the tan he had developed over the past few days, his tousled hair, and dressed in a white linen suit, he was visually everything she wanted. For the first time, she was doubting her desire to destroy him and seize the spoils of the de Passioné business failures. She tried to push the thought from her mind.

Claude's mannerisms and personality had changed since she had surreptitiously drugged him, however, there was one thing she wondered about. Incorrectly, Vicky had assumed the Viagra would increase Claude's desire, not fully understanding its true function. Unlike other sexual desire-enhancing drugs, Viagra treated only one problem.

She had expected a more pronounced effect from the liquid Viagra she had been feeding him. If there was an effect, he wasn't showing it toward her. She decided to check the dosage rather than waste an opportunity with the handsome creature who stood beside her. She had expected the drug to drive an animal desire within him. She wondered whether the lack of desire was due to an incorrect dosage or Claude's willpower to resist. She had never known any man to resist her. This presented her with a challenge.

"Vicky, I feel like taking a stroll along the promenade before we dine at one of those exquisite little French restaurants."

"Claude, I love that idea. Let me dress. It will not take long. Let me pour you a wine, and you sit here and relax while I change."

Claude eased himself into the luxurious lounger and relaxed. Vicky soon emerged with two wine glasses and a bottle of chilled Chablis.

She pulled up the other lounger and sat before pouring the wine.

"I thought you were going to change."

"Oh, but I will. Let's not waste this beautiful evening. An extra few minutes will not diminish the joy we will have this evening."

Already, Vicky's mind was racing ahead to the plan she had envisaged for the two of them.

Finally, the sky darkened. Vicky excused herself and left to change, emerging minutes later in a long, stylish white beach dress. She had swept her hair up and exposed her naked neck, upon which she wore a thin gold chain. Claude was amazed at the transformation. Gone was the somewhat ordinary but pretty woman. In front of him stood a striking beauty.

Claude stood and extended his hand to her.

"You look amazing. Let's take that stroll before we select a bistro."

Vicky purred with satisfaction, knowing she was capturing his interest.

"Yes, let's. I am looking forward to some of the fine cuisine those little restaurants are known for."

At that hour, the hotel lobby and grounds were quiet as guests were in their rooms preparing for dinner, or had already left the hotel to enjoy one of the many small French restaurants.

As they descended from the hotel's expansive lawn to the white sandy beach, Vicky slid her arm through Claude's. To the casual observer, they were just another vacationing couple without a care, which in reality was far from the truth.

A light cooling wind blew in from the ocean, reducing the feel of the day's humidity. The wind swept loose strands of Vicky's hair around her face. Claude watched and considered it a beautiful enhancement.

They walked the entire length of the beach before heading back to the old wooden stairs leading up to the restaurants. Vicky was pleased that the beach and promenade were almost deserted. She had no desire to engage in small talk with other couples, or in fact, anyone.

For the first time since 'capturing' Claude, she was feeling carefree. A dangerous situation, given her involvement with the major crime and what the syndicate was planning, and it was her plan. If she knew of the scheming and clandestine plans of certain others, she would not have been so casual about her situation.

Soft lights shone through the windows of a quaint bistro with an external deck looking out to sea. Claude looked up at the artistically carved wooden sign displaying the bistro's name…. 'Belle Époque'. He gently tugged Vicky's arm and gestured her into the restaurant. The maître d'hôtel welcomed them and, after enquiring, escorted them to a sheltered table on the outside deck at the rear. The rear deck was separated from the interior of the main restaurant by a large floor-to-ceiling glass window, which afforded the patrons inside a majestic view of the ocean and beach.

The maître d'hôtel signaled a waiter, who promptly arrived at the table and assisted Vicky in sitting at the table. Vicky loved the romantic charm and décor. Claude waited until she was settled and then sat across from her.

"This is magnificent. It reminds me of some of the bistros back in my native France. I wonder whether they have any of my favorite de Passioné Estates wine in their cellar?"

The mention of de Passioné snapped Vicky back into reality. She cursed the thought of what was about to transpire. Her emotions for Claude had grown, and now, for the first time, she felt the conflict. She was jolted back into the present by the young French waiter who was reciting the recommended specials for that evening.

Before ordering, Claude inquired about the wine selection, and in particular, the selection of de Passioné wines. The waiter stopped speaking and called the sommelier to join them.

A rather rotund middle-aged jovial man with a ruddy face and an impressive head of silver hair arrived at the table. He quickly engaged Claude in conversation, extolling the qualities and hidden virtues of the many bottles of de Pasioné wines in the restaurant's cellar.

The sommelier's eyes widened, and he excitedly praised Claude's selection of the best de Passioné wine.

Claude laughed, enjoying the man's exuberant rendition of a wine-lover's chant.

The scene between Claude and the man caused Vicky to relax, and she found herself liking Claude even more.

The waiter returned to take their orders. Vicky ordered first.

"I would like the lobster thermidor, please."

"Excellent choice, madame. And, sir, have you chosen?"

"Yes. My choice is the beef tenderloin with pepper and mushroom sauce and a side of asparagus, baby new potatoes, and sautéed onions."

"Excellent. I will submit your orders. Now, may I recommend some wines?"

Over the meal, Claude and Vicky chatted amiably. The food was good, and Vicky enjoyed the company and the distraction from the events that would soon unfold. They sat in silence until the sommelier arrived and offered an after-dinner wine. Politely, Claude thanked the man and refused.

Minutes later, Vicky excused herself and left the table to visit the ladies' room. While she was gone, Claude summoned the waiter for the bill.

The waiter returned with the bill before Vicky returned. Claude reached into his jacket and took out his wallet from which he removed his Black American Express card. The waiter thanked him and left.

While walking back to the table, Vicky noticed the waiter in a hushed conversation with the sommelier. They were both talking rapidly and glancing at Claude frequently. She was confused until the sommelier hurried across to the table.

"Monsieur de Passioné. I had no idea. You are the heir to the famous de Passioné estates. What a pleasure to serve you. It is no wonder you had such knowledge of wines."

"Please relax. We both enjoyed your professional service this evening."

Claude looked over at Vicky. Her face was tight and drawn.

"Come, Claude. We must leave. You have caused us a problem. That credit card will soon be traced, and we will receive some unwanted company."

As she rose quickly from the table and gathered her purse, Claude looked at her, confused.

"I will explain back at the hotel."

Chapter 23

San Francisco International Airport

Grand Hyatt Hotel

Barry's day had been long. He had taken the evening flight from Charles De Gaulle Airport in Paris to San Francisco. His attempts at sleeping during the 11 hour flight were unsuccessful, though he did doze off several times. Barry's mind was too occupied with trying to understand the dynamics of all the events impacting the business and why Claude had mysteriously disappeared.

After the flight touched down, Barry checked into the Grand Hyatt Hotel at the airport. He had chosen that hotel as he was to meet with Denis Ricard from the French Consulate for the next day's afternoon flight to Tahiti and wanted to relax. He had thoughts and plans to discuss with Denis.

Barry glanced at his watch. He wanted to call the de Passioné headquarters and receive an update on any new developments. He decided to wait, as the 9-hour time difference would mean that the people to whom he wished to speak would not yet be at the office. He had avoided contacting the de Passioné offices in California. He did not want to involve the management there in the intricacies of the fiasco occurring in France, nor speculate on Claude's disappearance.

Frustrated, Barry checked into the hotel, showered, and decided to visit the hotel's restaurant for a light meal.

On the way to the restaurant, he stopped at the little gift shop and bookstore in the lobby and purchased the day's 'International Narrator' newspaper.

The restaurant was not busy. Most travelers had eaten earlier in the evening. Barry was shown to a booth overlooking the airport runways. He was pleased to have the privacy of the booth.

A young waitress arrived to take his order. Her bubbly enthusiasm cheered Barry. He needed some relief from all the dark thoughts of the business and Claude. He ordered a Cabernet Sauvignon and settled on the veal piccata and angel hair pasta for the main course. The young waitress subtly gave him a flirtatious look before leaving. Barry smiled and thought to himself, "I still have it. I'm still the stud."

Barry sat quietly, absent-mindedly watching planes taxiing. He ran different scenarios through his mind to try and understand the present situation. Nothing made sense.

His meal arrived, served by the same waitress who made her interest in the handsome Australian evident. Barry was flattered and thought, "If this were another time, and if I weren't married to my beautiful Yvette."

After the meal, Barry leaned back in the comfortable seating of the booth with his wine and picked up the paper. He scanned through the never-ending stories of the Middle East conflict, some accounts of political scandals breaking in Washington, along with gossip about movie actors and rock stars. Nothing new or exciting, he decided.

He flipped to the paper's small business news section. There at the bottom of the 2nd page was a headline that shocked him.

"*International Investment Firms Preparing Rescue Financing of French Winery and Distillery*"

Sources in the finance community have finally broken their silence and are discussing the inside rumors of a massive bailout of the assets of the de Passioné family businesses. The business interests of the de Passioné family are centuries old and include some of the wineries and vineyards that produce some of France's internationally acclaimed and prize-winning wines. More recently, the family acquired the operations of the Mondial Distillery, whose products include vodkas, rums, gins, and other spirits that have rocketed to success in recent times.

A syndicate of financiers has met to prepare this bailout. It is rumored to be headed by Sir Reginald Coxburn and Tantamore Capital. Other syndicate members include Arnie Jacobson, Finance of New York, and an unknown Chinese group.

It defies logic why, with such winning products as the wines and the Mondial products, the de Passioné business has fallen into such disarray.

This reporter has been tracking the recent disappearance of Claude de Passioné and the possibility that it is linked to these recent developments. Claude's whereabouts are unknown. He had recently fled from the island of Rarotonga in the Cook Islands after a dramatic marriage collapse. He was last known to have boarded a flight to Tahiti, after which he mysteriously disappeared.

Efforts to discuss events with the de Passioné family interest were met with 'No comment.' We will be staying with this story.

(From files Lucy Lastik. Your Business Press. London. UK.)

Barry furiously read the article and then the source and the journalist attributed to the report. It was not a name he recognized, but he froze when he realized the journalist was identified as being with a London, UK, news group.

Barry re-read the article in disbelief and felt his temper rising.

Barry exploded. He thumped his fists on the table and swore out loud. The few remaining diners in the restaurant turned and stared at him. The waitress ran to him, concerned.

"Can I help you, sir? Is something wrong?"

"You better bloody believe it. Please get me a glass of the best fucking scotch you have."

Seeing his distress only served to drive her interest in Barry to a higher level.

Barry gulped down the scotch before scribbling his signature across the bill to charge the meal to his room. He rose from the table and, in a great rush, headed to his room to call the head office in France. He did not see the waitress write his room number on a napkin and slide it into her pocket.

In his room, Barry looked at the time but decided the information contained in the newspaper article justified the early morning awakening that Buzz Kutz was about to receive.

At the de Passioné residence, all was quiet. There had been a light snowfall overnight. The gardens and grounds were blanketed in snow, which muffled the normal sounds of birds and life. Except for a solitary light shining from the kitchen window, the residence was still. The only movement was that of the kitchen staff who were preparing breakfast for Buzz and Marie-France.

The shrill ringing of the de Passioné private phone pierced the bedroom's silence. Buzz grumbled as he rolled from the bed.

"Who the fuck has the nerve to call us this early on our private number?"

He snatched the decorative antique phone from its cradle."Kutz here. Who is this?"

Barry didn't wait for any pleasantries. He immediately launched into a tirade, accusing the newspaper of publishing damaging information and blaming the employees or others hired in sensitive roles at the company for leaking information.

"Well, greetings to you as well. I think you need to calm down. Please read me the whole article. I have not seen or heard about this, but I am sure the media will blitz us today."

Buzz listened as Barry read the article.

"Barry, that disclosure of the planned actions of Tantamore and Arnie Jacobson could not have been leaked by any of our people. It seems that this has been planted by one of them. It seems no coincidence that today Sir Reginald and Lady Thwacker arrive here for the visit that Marie-France had arranged."

"Shit. Buzz, you must take every precaution to prevent him from having access to any information or contact with our people. Make it as unpleasant for him as possible. Work on Marie-France and convince her to take them on a trip. Suggest the country estate. She loves it there."

" I am going to contact Horatio Henderson with this news. I will gather the team and conference back with you in an hour or so."

As Barry hung up, there was a soft knock at his door. He opened it to find the young waitress standing there smiling and no longer in her uniform.

Chapter 24

Fratti residence, Calabria, Italy

Luigi Fratti looked at the two men sitting across from him at the conference table in his outer office. No one except his most loyal soldiers ever gained access to his private office, and these men were not.

Luigi sat quietly after greeting the men, asking them to state their business. There was an awkward silence.

"I granted you both this meeting. I am busy, so if you have something to say or ask, then go ahead, or leave."

The taller, thin man with chiselled facial features and long black greasy hair pulled tight in a bun was the first to speak.

"Signore Fratti, thank you for taking your time to hear us. We have problems. You had promised a continual supply of products from the Chinese. The last two months have been bad. We barely received enough to satisfy our local market. My men in Rome and the other larger cities are angry and placing demands on us that we cannot meet. Some of the other gangs with South American contacts are taking away customers. We need more deliveries from you."

Silence filled the room. Luigi viewed them while deciding on his response.

" I am aware of the recent problems we have experienced. I am sure you know that the Americans, Dutch, and French have been aggressive in intercepting shipments from China. We have recently concluded several arrangements with suppliers, and very soon you will benefit from those. We are actively working on an opportunity in Europe that will allow us to distribute without the risk of interference by authorities. This should happen in the next month and resolve the problems we have had with shipping."

The second man shuffled forward and rested his hands and arms on the table.

Luigi appraised him. He was Hispanic, young and fit, and well-groomed.

"Signore Luigi, my people may have a solution to your problems here, and I am authorized to request a meeting between you and your people, with my organization. You will not be disappointed. We successfully established a new transportation system through Rotterdam, but let's discuss all that when we all meet."

"You are impertinent to come here, and without knowing me or the organizations I control, insinuate you have something better to offer. Soon you will all be asking me for help."

"My apologies. I did not mean to insult you, but to see if we can mutually benefit each other."

"What are you proposing? I don't need to wait and hear it from others in your operation. If you cannot speak to me of this, then we have no further business, as it seems that you do not have the authority or power to speak or make agreements on behalf of your people."

Luigi examined the man further. He was maybe 39 years old, and his physique indicated that of a person who exercised and worked out frequently. Beads of perspiration dotted the man's forehead, and heavy sweat stained beneath his armpits. Luigi sensed a trap and reached for the remote he had carried into the meeting. He pressed the button, and within seconds, several burly guards burst into the room with guns drawn.

"Both of you should have thought very carefully before attempting to fool me. Now you will pay the consequences."

The guards rushed and detained the men.

"Señor Valquez, you must be stupid to think I would not recognize you or understand the purpose of the meeting. My family and I have controlled regions of Italy for hundreds of years. You must be deranged to think we would allow a simple supply problem from our long-term suppliers to change that. You both made a fatal mistake, as you will soon find out."

"Please Signore, wait. We are here to try and make a simple business arrangement. There was no harm or disrespect intended."

"We do not need or want the involvement of you Colombians here in my business in Italy. Especially in my business."

Luigi turned away to leave the room, instructing his men.

"You know what needs to be done."

Luigi went to the credenza in his office and removed a bottle of wine. As he uncorked it, he smiled as the sound of the shots echoed around his office.

Sitting behind his desk, he reflected on the meeting. He was concerned that a rival gang dared to request a meeting at his office. He wondered about the presence of the Hispanic who had ventured the opinion that a solution to the supply problems could be handled by them. The idea of a rival gang providing any product riled Luigi. It was obvious to him that the Hispanic was sent by one of the South American cartels. With the Hispanic now dead, Luigi realized days of danger lay ahead for him and his gang members. He decided he needed to take action. He reached for his phone and punched in the numbers to Arnie Jacobson's secure phone. After several rings, the phone was answered.

"Who is this?"

"Arnie, it is me, Luigi."

"What is so important that you are calling me?"

"I have just had an unfortunate meeting here in my office. It seems our supply problem has become known amongst others in our business. Seems they want in and to supply us. One of the attendees was representing certain South American interests. They had the cojones to come to my office with their proposal. We have avoided any confrontation with them in the past. They are dangerous and bring bad luck. I am worried that our venture could get compromised if we don't move fast."

"Luigi, my friend. Relax. We leaked information to the media a day ago. The news has been picked up and made its way into many influential newspapers. Our phones here in New York have not stopped ringing. We seeded the information with the claim that a white knight investor is working with us to bail out the target. My UK partner, Sir Reginald's firm, is mentioned as partnering with us. It will only be a matter of time before the major banks and lenders will be demanding more information from us. They will be eager to either pull out their investments or loans. We will, of course, play along with them, and at the appropriate time, we will announce the deal as dead. That announcement will be made after the lenders have reached an agreement to have their loans or investments paid out of the proceeds of the new financing. After the deal is announced as dead, we expect the banks to foreclose and demand full repayment. At that time, we will move in. The stocks will have been suspended from trading during the possible refinancing, and after we make our announcement, they will be worthless. That is when we move in and take all of the de Passioné family businesses. We will keep it operating, resolve the operational problems, and return the businesses to profitability before selling them. We will sell all the businesses except for the laboratory operations of Mondial. It is already set up as a separate company and offers testing of products to others. The management of the laboratory will change, and our Chinese partners will move in to manufacture the products you so badly need."

"Arnie, I expect things will heat up here now. Both of the men they sent to me are now dead."

"Luigi, that was a stupid move. It is impossible to speed up the process. I suggest you make their remains go missing. Don't do the typical mob thing and dump them to be found as a message to the other mobs. Use your head. There is a lot at stake now."

" I will ensure that the bodies can never be found."

"Luigi, there is something else you need to know. That fool Sir Reginald has gone on vacation for a week with one of his twisted love interests. Bad timing."

"I don't understand. He is entitled to a vacation. He is in constant contact with us. In fact, it may look good to others."

"No. Not where he has gone. He has gone to stay at the de Passioné residence. His love interest is a relative of that crazy Marie-France de Passioné. He could create major problems, but I intend to have him distracted. Soon, he will wish he had never taken that trip to France."

Chapter 25

Tahiti Noveau Hotel and Resort, Papette, Tahiti.

The after-dinner stroll along the beach to their hotel invigorated Claude. As they walked, he studied Vicky. She intrigued him. He wondered about her position as a financial manager for Tantamore, one of Britain's notable finance and banking firms. Her manner defied the image of a banker, yet she knew the language and system. In the early evening light, she radiated a unique beauty that Claude found hard to resist.

It was now the second day that Vicky had not drugged Claude, and the results were apparent. He was alert and seemed to be paying more attention to her. What Claude did not know was that she had a similar attraction to him, and in her mind, she was scheming to manipulate him into her bed.

She kicked off her shoes and walked down to the water's edge, deliberately wetting her dress and pulling Claude into the shallow water. Together they laughed and pretended to splash each other. Vicky experienced a euphoric feeling and was anxious to return to the hotel. She had plans.

Claude ran up behind her and scooped her up into his arms, and jokingly pretended to throw her into the water. She shrieked in mock fear.

They continued to playfully tease each other until they reached their hotel. Vicky decided it was time to attempt the seduction.

"Claude, it is still early. There is no way I would sleep if I went to bed. Besides, I am feeling too alive to retire. I don't want to sit in the hotel bar. I want to go and change out of these wet clothes and enjoy some wine. Will you join me?"

Claude hesitated but then decided to join her. He was feeling much more alive and better over the last two days. He decided he needed this break after all the stress of events in Rarotonga. He accepted.

"First, I will go to my room and change into something cooler. The clothes I wore for dinner are too warm for this climate. Give me a few minutes, and I will meet you in your room."

While Claude was changing, Vicky poured two glasses of the finest de Passioné wine. She then went into her bathroom and removed the vial containing the liquid Viagra. Careful not to overdose, Claude, she poured the exact dosage into the wine, then returned with the glasses and placed them on the low coffee table in the living room.

Satisfied, she slipped into her bedroom to change.

Time slipped by, and Vicky became concerned that Claude had not returned. She was about to go to his room when there was a loud knock at the door. Frowning, she went to open the door. No one on the island knew of her presence. A young man dressed in a bellman's uniform stared at the scantily clad woman who opened the door. He stammered about several urgent messages he was delivering. Vicky turned back into the room, scooped up some money off the counter, and thrust it into his hand.

She looked at the messages. Each was on a folded slip of hotel paper and stapled shut for confidentiality.

Several were from Sir Nigel and two from Arnie Jacobson. Sir Nigel's second message expressed his frustration that she was not answering her secure phone. It then continued stating that plans had moved ahead faster than planned, but with complications. She opened the messages from Arnie Jacobson. They read the same as Sir Nigel and requested her to contact him urgently. For the first time, she felt a slight resentment that the time she planned with Claude was about the be interrupted. While the project she had planned was huge and financially beneficial to her, she wondered whether Claude had become more important to her.

As she stood pondering her situation, the door opened and Claude entered. He had changed his clothing and was wearing a lightweight shirt and shorts. She smiled as she looked at his tanned figure.

"Claude, let's sit outside for a little. I have poured you a wine that I am sure you are familiar with."

Outside on the patio, Claude asked her what she had intended to tell him once they were back at the hotel.

"Claude, at the restaurant, you gave away your identity. The waiter now knows it is you, and not the name you used to check into the hotel. In addition, you used your credit card. Your desire to be anonymous here has now been destroyed. Within no time, you can expect the media to arrive looking for Claude de Passioné….of the famous French family. Your days of enjoying a quiet vacation are over."

"I never thought about that."

" I have received messages from my office. It appears I am needed there to resolve a crisis with a financing. I will probably leave the next day. But until then, let us enjoy our time together. Will you stay here now your cover is exposed?"

"No. Maybe I will go with you to the UK and then back to France."

That was not the news Vicky wanted to hear. They needed Claude away from the company while executing the project. If he became aware of the situation and interfered, it could jeopardize the whole operation.

Vicky remained silent for several minutes, thinking about the situation. She felt trapped and needed time to think of a plan to keep Claude away from the business.

"Vicky, you have gone quiet. Is everything OK?"

"Yes. I am just enjoying the evening here with you."

Claude reached over and caressed her shoulder. She leaned toward him.

"Vicky, I will be lonely here without you. I have developed emotions for you. If you can't stay, then I will find a way to be near you."

"I will know more after I call them, but that will be in the morning. Tonight we will just enjoy our time."

Vicky stood and extended a hand to Claude and gently tugged him back inside. Claude sensed an excitement run through him and was aware of his erection. The liquid Viagra had hit.

Once inside, Vicky forcibly threw her hands around Claude's neck and launched into a long, passionate kiss. Claude felt a huge pressure building inside him, and he pulled Vicky tightly against him. Every contour of his body pressed firmly against her, and she reciprocated by taking her hand from his neck and running it down his chest, strumming her fingers against his naked skin. She pulled back from Claude and, with exact precision, released her flimsy top and then her sheer panties.

Vicky stood naked in front of him. Claude stood mesmerized with his enlarged penis throbbing and studied her fine naked form. While he had previously wondered about Vicky's figure, her clothing had disguised her true voluptuous figure.

Claude reached forward and placed his hands on each of her shoulders. He then slid his hands down her body. As his hands moved down her body and over her erect nipples, she shuddered at the feeling of the tingling electric sensation generated by the palms of his hands. His hands continued lower. Vicky pulled back and dragged him into the bedroom. The lovemaking was hungry and fast. Her Latino heritage and passion were unbridled.

Claude's stamina, enhanced by the Viagra, drove her to unimaginable heights.

Exhausted, Claude rolled over in the bed beside her. He looked into her eyes and smiled.

"You certainly are a surprise. I hope your appetite still hungers for me."

Claude threw his arm across her naked waist and pulled her on top of him. Within seconds, Vicky wildly rocked on him while he thrust and groaned. Minutes passed before they both collapsed laughing. Exhausted, Claude drifted into a sleep.

Vicky lay with her head on Claude's chest, listening to the rapid and loud beating of his heart. Suddenly, she was overcome with emotion and conflicting waves of concern for Claude. She looked at him as he slept. The thought of the agony and problems he would endure, as a result of her plan, started to torment her. Her mind drifted to the immense wealth she would gain and then to a vision of a life with Claude. The fleeting idea of stopping the project entered her mind. She quickly realized the impossibility of abandoning it. The others would exact a fatal revenge. She was trapped between her greed and emotions, but the idea of the freedom the wealth would give her played against her new emotions.

Chapter 26

Barry's eventful night. Grand Hyatt Hotel

San Francisco International Airport

The gentle knocking at his hotel room door continued. Barry opened the door to find the young waitress standing and smiling. With her waitressing uniform gone. With lightly applied makeup, she was extremely beautiful.

"Can I help you? Why are you here?"

"Good evening, Mr. Jones. I wanted to check on you after the incident in the restaurant this evening. You were very distressed, and I was concerned for you and worried that trouble might come to you."

"Miss, I appreciate your concern, but no, it was just some bad news that was incorrect and angered me. I am sorry if I created a scene."

"No. We have seen a lot worse, but my concern was for you and what happened after you left the restaurant."

"What do you mean?"

"A man was asking a lot of questions about you."

Barry frowned and was immediately concerned.

"Maybe you should come in and tell me about that."

He opened the door and directed her to the suite's living area.

"My name is Barry. What is yours?"

"I am Fleur Leclair."

"Please sit, Fleur. That is a nice name. I am married to a French lady. Her name is Yvette. Now tell me about this man who was asking questions."

"He showed me an identification that claimed he was a reporter for a television network. He said he was researching matters for a segment called 'Business Today.' He was persistent and aggressive. I did not like him and was therefore concerned for you."

"I am going to pour myself a drink while I listen to what happened. Would you care for a drink now you are no longer working?"

"Yes, I would love a Chablis if that is possible."

Barry proceeded to the room's bar and poured her a drink and a large whiskey for himself. He returned and sat opposite Fleur.

"Tell me what happened."

"He was with one of the large US networks. For some reason, he seemed to believe I had information about you. I tried to explain I had never seen you before. He was adamant that I knew you and some others traveling with you. He was angry when I told him you were just a guest here at the hotel. He thrust this card into my hand and asked me to contact him if I found out anything about what you were doing and any others with you."

Fleur handed a cream colored business card to Barry. It read:

Marcus Horowitz, Investigative Reporter, Business Today, International News Broadcasting. New York.

Barry recalled watching him on a newscast regarding offshore investing, and how, watching the clip, he had formed a dislike for the man. He found Horowitz's editorial allegations far-reaching and speculative while accusing many innocent investors.

"Fleur, I appreciate you coming and telling me about this. Did he happen to mention any names of people he thought were with me?"

"He did, but I don't remember."

Barry sat back in his chair and observed her. She was young, beautiful, and intelligent. She was not as young as she had appeared under the soft lighting of the restaurant. In the brighter light of his room, she appeared older. He estimated she was twice the age he had assumed.

"Fleur, I am curious why you are working as a waitress."

"I am a student at the University here. I need to make some money."

"Excuse me for being direct, but you appear a little older to be a student. Did you travel or take time to explore another career, and then decide to attend university?"

"No, I had met someone after graduation. We were very close, and our relationship grew over several years. We were about to get married and start a family. A month before the planned wedding, I found he was unfaithful and had proposed to another woman. I left and hid with my parents for two years. I was shattered. I started University at an older age."

"I am sorry. I did not mean to pry into your personal life."

"May I ask Barry, where are you traveling to? Is it far or somewhere exciting?"

"I am on my way to Tahiti. Business."

"No, are you serious? I am from Tahiti. My family is there. I was born in France, and we moved when my father accepted a position there. My father, Pierre, is a director in the security forces there. How strange. My mother owns a fashion boutique at Papette Airport, which specializes in French couture. This must be a fate."

Barry could not believe his luck. A possible name and introduction to the correct authority in Tahiti."I would like to meet your father. He might be able to assist me in my business there."

"I am sure he will help you if it is an area in which he is able. What is your business in Tahiti?"

Barry sat quietly, wondering whether he should discuss the nature of his trip to Tahiti. While thinking about whether to tell her of Claude's disappearance, Barry's phone rang. He snatched the phone and answered. It was Buzz Kutz.

"Barry, I don't know if you have access to all satellite channels at the hotel, but I suggest you find one that has access to International News Broadcasting. They are broadcasting a news special on the de Passioné family and businesses in 15 minutes. That sleaze bag analyst, Debbie Pouch, intends to update the world with the 'scandals rocking the Passioné family and the mysterious disappearance of Claude.' I have no idea what muck they have racked up, but I suggest you watch it. I have already contacted our lawyers. Horatio returned from his New York trip and is on his way here to watch it with me."

"Shit, just want we don't need. The sensationalist press is about to create false drama. I will watch it and call you back."

Barry stood and poured himself another whiskey, along with a wine for Fleur. He decided to fill her in on the trip and the details of Claude's disappearance.

"Fleur, what I am about to tell you should not be discussed with others. Can you assure me of that?"

"Yes, I will keep it in confidence," she nodded.

"Are you familiar with the de Passioné family and their business?"

"Yes, in fact, my father always served the de Passioné wines when entertaining or at dinners. He loved the wines."

"The reason for my trip to Tahiti is that Claude de Passioné is missing. He had left the island of Rarotonga and flown to Tahiti. There are records of him departing Rarotonga, but no corresponding arrival info for him in Tahiti. He has simply disappeared. At the same time, the de Passioné wine and spirits businesses are being sabotaged by unknown parties. I am going to Tahiti in an attempt to find him."

Fleur sat wide-eyed as Barry continued and detailed the troubles and events of the recent past.

"I am sure my father can assist you in your search. He is in a senior position and has access to all police and traveler information. I can call him before and tell him of your situation."

"I need to watch this news. You are welcome to stay and watch it with me."

"I would like that."

Barry returned to the bar and poured himself a large whiskey. He was sure he would need it to quell the fury he anticipated the newscast would generate. With the whiskey in his hand, he sank back into the luxurious couch and flipped through channels until he found the International News Broadcasting channel. The network's logo of a spinning globe dotted with small green dollar signs faded out, and the camera focused on the news desk where a female and male newsreader sat. When the blaring trumpet music faded, the female, who was heavily made up and had the appearance of a toy doll, led in with an announcement.

"Good evening. Tonight's lead story is the rapidly unfolding deterioration of the historic wine empire of the French powerhouse, the de Passioné family. Later in the broadcast, we will be joined by investigative reporter Marcus Horowitz, who is on the ground in San Francisco, and Debbie Pouch, our financial analyst, to help us understand all that is happening with this. San Francisco is not far from the de Passioné California vineyards and winery, and earlier, we sought answers there but were refused. But first, the story. Over to you, Chris."

"Thank you, Cecily. I think we need to review the de Passioné legacy for our viewers, and I have prepared a brief video of the history and players in this saga. Firstly, a little of the recent history."

The TV screen flashed, and the image of a stately-looking man appeared.

"This is the Marquis de Passioné. He was the driving force behind the successful expansion of the business over the past 25 years. The de Passioné family has for centuries been involved in wine-making and the cultivation of vineyards in France. Under the Marquis, he was instrumental in expanding the operations into Italy and Spain and establishing the brand in the International market. His business acumen was beyond question, however, his social activities and philandering led to an untimely death when a jealous husband stumbled upon him in a moment of passion with the man's wife. After his death, the business was to be inherited by his son Claude. There had been bad blood between father and son, and Claude embarked upon university studies and International travel. He only returned to the business under some duress at the request of his mother, Marie-France. The growth of the business slowed as Claude's passion for the family business was lacking. Later, he would make changes that corrected that. I will address that later in the presentation. Now we move on."

Again, the screen flashed, and a front-on picture of a heavily made-up Marie-France wearing a hideous lime green dress appeared. The picture had been taken in her younger years when she was an avid hippie. Long beaded necklaces with peace symbol ceramic pendants hung from her neck. She wore Jesus sandals with high leather strappings wound around each leg that extended to her knees. Over her shoulder was an Indian shawl.

Now, my dear viewers, this is the eccentric Marie-France de Passioné. Her interests were never in the wine business. Like her husband, the Marquis, her interests ran to adventures with very young members of the opposite sex. Marie-France has never played an active role in the de Passioné business. She has been a benefactor to many charities and causes, some quite bizarre. But overall, this strange woman has been an influence on her son, Claude. Next is Buzz Kutz."

The picture of a uniformed young Buzz radiated from the screen.

"This is Buzz Kutz. A bit of a mystery in the whole de Passioné puzzle. He is the husband of Marie-France, the son of an extremely wealthy industrialist who owned companies producing products for IBM, GE, Ford, and others. Buzz inherited a fortune but moved away from the business to pursue a career with our spook forces, the FBI and CIA, and God knows what else. He shunned corporate life and, for a while, was in the entertainment business as a country and western singer. He is fiercely dedicated to the family and

Marie-France. At de Passioné businesses, he is the senior operations man and looks after all of the company and family security. And now, we have Claude."

A picture of Claude appeared. He was dressed in tropical, carefree clothing and portrayed the image of a wealthy playboy. Barry muttered his disapproval of the picture.

"And here we have Claude de Passioné, the heir to a fortune worth billions. A globe-trotting, wealthy playboy with mistresses in tropical locations. Claude left the family Chateau in France for an education at the Sorbonne. This is where his life changed. In those early years, he became involved with an International smuggling ring. Later, he was involved with many women in different countries, many of whom would still like to see him brought to justice. As Claude matured, he attracted some exceptional vintners to the business, and he immersed himself in the business, but he alone wasn't responsible for the amazing success of de Passioné wines. He hired Barry Jones. My next topic."

A portrait of Barry filled the screen. It was an old picture. In the picture, Barry stood grinning and wearing an old Australian diggers hat and a military shirt. There was a look of mischief on his face.

"Now this is Barry Jones, the wild Australian who has applied his fine Australian winemaking techniques for the benefit of the de Passioné family. Barry is Claude's right-hand man in business and personal matters. He is highly respected within the industry."

The sight of himself on TV and wearing his 'down under clothes cracked Barry up. He howled with laughter. Fleur looked at him as if he had gone mad.

" Well, that's it from me. As our viewers can see, this is a dysfunctional, wealthy, spoiled family. Back to you, Cecily."

"Thank you, Chris. Now let's bring on Debbie and Marcus. Welcome to you both."

"Hi, Cecily. While Marcus has been out enjoying San Francisco, I have been investigating and interviewing people intimately involved in this whole de Passioné scandal, and frankly, Cecily, what is emerging isn't a pretty picture. My research team and I have spent hours attempting to get answers from some of the suppliers of de Passioné and Mondial, their wildly successful distillery company. What we found out was that a pattern of recurring problems existed. These problems included late payments, nonacceptance of orders for no reason, intimidation, and requests for bribes to continue as a supplier. Many of these suppliers have been long-term vendors to de Passioné. Many of those we spoke with raised serious questions regarding the disappearance of Claude de Passioné, and many spoke of the problems they experienced over the past 6 months in contacting him or his senior people. Now Claude is missing. What we know is that Claude was involved in a nasty marital breakup at his home on Rarotonga in the Cook Islands. From all accounts, it was a particularly bad breakup. Claude fled the island, abandoning his wife and daughter. We understand that Claude had only recently discovered in the past year that he had fathered a daughter. It seems that Claude had had affairs with several Polynesian women, and it was during this period of careless behavior that he fathered this innocent child."

In the room, Barry became angry and cursed at the TV, proclaiming that it was all lies and fabricated to create a drama to entice viewers to want more and to turn against Claude and the family. He was angry.

"To continue, Cecily, there is a lot more to this story. This afternoon, I was able to contact and interview Arnie Jacobson, whose firm, Arnie Jacobson Hedge Funds, has been mentioned as a major player in the rescue efforts to save the de Passioné businesses. Here is a clip of the interview."

A video appeared on the screen and focused on the rotund profile of Arnie Jacobson, who professed that he had little to offer. He then wondered whether Claude had fled in an attempt to avoid inquiries into financial mismanagement, including the siphoning off of corporate funds. Arnie continued and expressed serious concern that he expected a possible failure of the firm if Claude wasn't found and if the consortium of investment bankers refused to extend a further financial lifeline.

Barry was furious. He saw how the lies had been fabricated to disparage Claude, the family, and those involved with the business. The TV coverage continued.

"Thank you, Debbie. That certainly sounds bad for the company. And now we have some comments from Marcus."

"Yes, Cecily. I am here in San Francisco. As mentioned earlier, we have tried to get someone in authority at de Passioné for an interview, but our requests were declined. I have been investigating and have uncovered some interesting facts. I have uncovered that Barry Jones is here in San Francisco with others and on his way to Tahiti. Our inquiries in Rarotonga confirm that Claude de Pasioné took a flight from the island to Tahiti, but officials in Tahiti claim to have no record of him arriving there. This is most peculiar, and with everything that is happening adds to the air of suspicion that Claude is possibly involved in some criminal activity related to the current financial mess of the companies. It certainly raises serious doubts about the de Passioné family. We will keep you updated and now back to you in the studio, Cecily."

Barry flicked off the TV. Fleur sat looking at him.

"It is all lies, Fleur. There are indeed attempts being made to sabotage the business, and we need to find out why and who is manipulating this. For something of this scale, it has to be someone major and with a lot of influence."

"I will call my Dad. I am sure if Claude is in Tahiti, he will help find him. Now I must go. Give me your contact information, and I will send you the way to contact him."

As Fleur left, the phone rang. Buzz and Horatio came on the line once Barry answered.

Buzz was beside himself.

"All fucking lies. We will sue those bastards when this is over. Both the reporters and that network."

"Buzz, I will be on the flight tomorrow. I am working on some ideas and will contact you once I land in Tahiti."

Chapter 27

Flight to Tahiti.

Barry had woken feeling fresh, but still annoyed at the biased and inaccurate TV news coverage. He spent the morning speaking with Buzz and Horatio on matters related to the business. After lunch at the hotel, he took a shuttle to the airport to await the arrival of his traveling companion, Denis Ricard, to join him on the afternoon flight to Tahiti. While checking out of the hotel, the Front Desk handed a neatly addressed envelope to him. He opened it to find a handwritten note from Fleur advising him she had spoken to her father and advised him of Barry and the nature of his trip. Her father, Pierre Leclair, had agreed to meet, and she had included contact information.

Barry was looking forward to the conversation with Denis. It would be a welcome relief from the days of intense and depressing discussions relating to the de Passioné business. Barry was pleased to be away from the business. He needed a change of environment to allow him to gather his thoughts and analyze the situation without the constant interruptions related to the crisis.

While he waited for Denis, Barry visited the airport store and bought several national newspapers. Eager to find out what the media was saying, he found a coffee shop and settled in to read the papers.

An hour had passed, and Barry checked the time. It was close to the time he had agreed to meet Denis at the Departures entrance of the International Passenger Terminal.

Barry gathered his items and papers and sauntered to the entrance.

After the TV report from Marcus Horowitz, Barry was wary and checked around for the presence of any possible reporters or photographers. He did not need to have his meeting with Denis exposed.

Barry positioned himself beside a kiosk selling travel insurance. From there, he had a view of cars dropping off passengers at the entrance door. He did not have to wait long before Denis arrived. A black Mercedes limo pulled up to the curb. The driver jumped from his seat, then proceeded to the rear passenger door and opened it. As he did so, one of the traffic wardens started shouting and blowing a piercing whistle.

"You can't stop there. It is for drop-off only. You cannot leave the car. You must stay in it at all times. Return to the car immediately, or I will ticket you."

The driver, who was a security officer, turned and snarled at the warden.

"This is a high-security diplomatic passenger. We have the privilege to stop here until my passenger is safely inside."

The warden swore and begrudgingly left to victimize the next car.

Barry watched as Denis emerged from the car and was quickly escorted by the burly driver into the terminal. He started to walk over and called Denis by name. The driver/security person spun and stared at Barry.

"Don't worry. He is with me. We are traveling together."

The security man relaxed, and as he did, a woman in a dark blue uniform hurried toward them. She introduced herself as the head of airport security for VIP passengers and invited Denis and Barry to accompany her to a private lounge. Barry loved the attention. He hated traveling with the masses.

In the lounge, Denis laughed and welcomed Barry. The security woman took their travel documents and arranged for their small amount of baggage to be taken and checked onto the flight.

"So, my friend Barry. It seems that your life is chaotic these days. I saw that TV report last night. The channel ran it several times throughout the evening. I guess that is one way to become famous."

"It is not the way I wish to become famous. A lot of it was inaccurate or lies made up by the reporter to enhance the story. We will be taking legal action against them when this is all solved."

"You can tell me more during the flight. Right now it's afternoon and it is time for a nice relaxing glass of wine before the flight."

Denis and Barry sat chatting and enjoying their drinks until the lounge concierge advised them it was time to board their flight. She offered to drive them to their gate in the little electric cart, a service provided as part of the private lounge.

Barry was delighted. A long walk through the airport was not something he had looked forward to.

At the gate, they exited the vehicle. The woman smiled and handed them their boarding passes and travel documents.

They settled into their seats in the 1st Class cabin of the plane, and within a minute, a flight attendant arrived with champagne flutes and a bottle of chilled Bollinger champagne.

Barry was impressed

"Bloody corker service from this bunch. Sure beats traveling cattle class on some of these airlines."

"Barry, we need to be comfortable as this is a 9-hour flight and can get tedious."

Time slipped by until the whine of the engines being started, and a slight jolt shook the plane as they pushed back from the gate.

Denis raised his glass and toasted Barry.

"Well, here's to a successful trip for us both."

The jet's engines whined louder, and the plane accelerated down the runway before it lifted and climbed steeply. Barry looked out the cabin window and took in the view of the sun setting in the west over the Pacific Ocean. He experienced a premonition that the trip would be successful. As he was thinking of everything that had happened, Denis reached over and tapped his arm.

"Tell me more about this situation. I am not sure that what I have read in the papers or seen on TV is accurate. What is the real story?"

"You are correct. There is a lot more that we have kept quiet. This fiasco seemed to start after we arranged financing to take over and purchase Mondial, which has proven to be an excellent decision. The profits and growth have exceeded our expectations. The distillery operations have grown at a faster annual rate than our wine business."

Denis listened intently as Barry described the events that had disrupted the company's operations. He did not interrupt Barry.

An hour passed, and Barry paused when a flight attendant offered them hors d'oeuvres.

"Barry, based on what you have described to me, it would appear the disruptions are planned and not coincidental. Someone with powerful connections is orchestrating this. Do you suspect the disappearance of Claude is tied into this?"

"I have wondered. I cannot determine any link. My conviction is that the problems are related to that financing. It almost seems that someone is deliberately attempting to sabotage the business and cause it to fail. If Claude is missing, then the control of the company passes to Marie-France, and I have little confidence she is capable of managing and saving it from failure."

"There are security and intelligence people I work with in Tahiti. If you agree, I will arrange a meeting for you to attend and brief them about all of this. They have local contacts with certain underworld figures. If anyone has talked about Claude, I am sure that info would have filtered through to them. Have you initiated contact with any private investigators or others?"

"No, but I had an interesting encounter with a young lady from Tahiti at the hotel. She told me about her father and arranged for me to meet him. He works for the French government in security in Tahiti."

"That is interesting. What is his name?"

"His name is Pierre Leclair."

Denis laughed.

"That is so funny. He works with me. He is a member of the DGSE (Directorate-General for External Security), a part of the French Intelligence Services. Their role is to obtain security information on any threat to the security of France. They work with two other security forces who mainly deal with internal threats. I think Pierre would be a good person for you to discuss the situation with. The de Passioné businesses are important in the French culture and economy. DGSE or DGSI will be most interested in any attempt to sabotage an important French company. They have the power to investigate the sources behind any threats. These are very high-profile secret services and have approval from the highest levels of government to take action to protect our interests. I suggest you arrange to meet Pierre before taking any action yourself. He will direct you to the best sources."

Barry considered Denis. He remembered his earlier dealings with the French authorities in Tahiti and was concerned he would receive the same indifferent treatment.

"Denis, in the past, when we needed help, the assistance was marginal. I hope that this time, that will not be the case. We encountered extreme arrogance."

"Unfortunately, we have some employees here from Paris, and they have brought their Parisian arrogance with them. I do not think you will be treated that way, as you will be assisted by Pierre Leclair, and his authority is widely respected. He is not the person to upset. He is a powerful force and not to be taken lightly."

Their conversation lapsed, and both Barry and Denis drifted to sleep for the balance of the flight.

Upon arrival, Barry and Denis retrieved their luggage and headed to the airport exit. Denis was met by a woman from the French consulate who had been sent to escort him to the residences used for visiting consular officials.

Denis shook hands with Barry and arranged to meet him the next day.

Barry had observed an individual who seemed to be paying particular interest in them. He tried but could not place the man who was tall with dark brown hair and a muscular physique. He looked familiar.

While waiting for the hotel shuttle, Barry noticed the man had followed him and appeared to be waiting for someone. Barry had no doubts he was being watched and followed.

Chapter 28

de Passioné Residence , France

Buzz's mood matched the cold, blowing, and snowy weather that was whipping France. The arrival of Lady Agnes Thwacker and Sir Reginald Coxburn from England, several days earlier, did nothing to improve his demeanor. His afternoon meeting with Horatio Henderson had not helped. It seemed the financial vultures were circling in advance of the failure of the de Passioné businesses. The consortium of bankers had been spooked by the recent media reports, and even the concerted efforts of Horatio and his team failed to allay their fears of failure and financial losses for them.

His annoyance had grown that afternoon when he discovered Sir Reginald Coxburn had been probing the staff at the residence in an attempt to gather information on Claude's whereabouts and learn of the spreading rumors.

The silence of the room was interrupted by a loud snap as the lock of the salon door was opened. Marie-France entered, leading Lady Agnes and Sir Reginald into the room.

"I hope you don't mind, but my dear friends here and I thought it would be nice to join you. We can all sit around that nice big fire you have burning here and enjoy some fine cognac to keep us warm on this miserable, cold afternoon. Reggie does so much enjoy his cognac."

Buzz smiled and nodded as he gestured to the luxurious chairs arranged in front of the stately marble fireplace.

"Certainly, my dear. Your cousin, Lady Agnes, is more than welcome to join me. After all, she is related to the British Royals, and who am I to turn one of them away? "

"You are so kind, Buzz."

They seated themselves in front of the crackling fire. Buzz gazed at Lady Agnes. He despised her. He disliked the phony, exaggerated high-society British accent and her appearance. As he watched, she pirouetted in front of the chair closest to the fire and made a sweeping gesture to Sir Reginald to take the chair next to her.

Buzz looked at the two of them and then at Marie-France. He wondered what he had allowed to happen to him, and decided he would soon find a way to excuse himself. His gaze returned to Lady Agnes. She was afflicted with the same poor sense of style as Marie-France but with a British twist. He took in her heavily made-up face, caked with some type of heavy makeup to hide any blemishes. Her hair was pulled back in a tight bun that seemed to stretch the skin on either side of her eyes. A string of large baroque pearls hung around her neck. Buzz chuckled to himself as he mentally thought of the sexual games Sir Reginald would play with them. She was wearing a military-style tunic over a drab brown blouse and a garish tartan skirt, from which her white skinny legs emerged, showing mid-length dark green stockings leading down into heavy boots.

His gaze then settled on Sir Reginald, with his sharp, pointed features and mouse-like eyes. There was nothing attractive about the man. When he spoke, his high-pitched, warbly voice drew attention to the quivering of his large Adam's apple and the spittle that formed on his bright red lips. For the visit, Sir Reginald had chosen clothing he assumed would be appropriate for a country squire to wear when visiting a vineyard and spending time in the country. He was dressed in a tweed blazer over a matching tweed waistcoat, with heavy Merino wool tapered shooting trousers.

Buzz decided Sir Reginald would regret his choice of clothing when he encountered the events planned for him.

"Let me have one of the servants fetch up some fine cognac. French, of course."

Sir Reginald was about to speak, but Buzz cut him off to address the servant.

"Johnson, could you please bring us 4 snifters and a bottle of Delamain XO Pale and Dry Cognac ?"

"Certainly, Sir."

Sir Reginald listened and thought to himself, " How can they afford a £900 bottle of fine cognac when the business is suffering so much? But, I will enjoy."

"I must say, Buzz, what an excellent choice of Cognac. You are to be congratulated for your knowledge."

Buzz saw the ideal opportunity to manipulate the situation, take control of Sir Reginald, and stop his snooping around the business.

"Sir Reginald, tomorrow I need to travel into the village for some business reasons. I would like it if you would accompany me. Besides, it's better than just sitting here inside with all this bad weather. You can visit some of the art galleries and stores there."

He had barely finished extending the invitation when Lady Agnes exclaimed.

"I would love to join you and visit those quaint stores. That excites me."

Buzz could not believe his luck. Now he could control them both and put his plan in place to encourage them to return to England and stop prying around for information on the issues the business was dealing with. This would be the first of the special events he had planned to convince Sir Reginald to decide on an early return to England.

"It will be my pleasure to show you the little village. Besides, in this weather, it will be a little boring here. It's impossible to enjoy the grounds of the estate. Tomorrow, I will drive us through some spectacular country. We will be gone for several hours. In the village, there is a special restaurant I would like to take you to enjoy."

Marie-France looked confused.

"Will I be joining you?"

"No, I think it is best you stay here in case we receive information regarding Claude."

As he spoke and mentioned Claude, he observed Sir Reginald's reaction. There was a discernible turn of the head and an expression of interest on Sir Reginald's face. The movement was not lost on Buzz.

"That is a very strange situation indeed. Lady Agnes and I have discussed Claude's disappearance. We do not understand where he could be."

"We are sure Claude has decided to take some private time for himself. The turmoil he went through in Rarotonga was extreme. He has endured a lot. I am convinced he will be in contact soon."

Knowing the true situation with Claude's disappearance, Sir Reginald was silently pleased that Buzz and the others did not suspect anything other than Claude taking private time for himself.

"I am sure you are correct, Buzz. Claude is a smart man. I suspect that any man who had to endure what he has would also want time to think and heal."

Buzz found Sir Reginald's comment to be disingenuous. He had noticed that since their arrival, both Lady Agnes and Sir Reginald had made conciliatory remarks about Claude. Buzz was convinced they both knew more, but were intent on discovering whether his absence was contributing to the problem with the business. Buzz could not exactly determine why they made such remarks.

"I am sure you are right, Sir Reginald. Now, if you can all excuse me, I have some business to look after before I retire for the night. I will not be joining you for dinner. Prepare for an exciting day tomorrow."

Buzz smiled as he thought of the plans he had in store for the guests and hoped they would decide on an early return to England.

The servant, Johnson, returned with 4 tulip-shaped snifters filled with the precious golden cognac. He handed each of them a glass from the tray he carried.

Buzz raised his glass and proposed a toast.

"Cheers and to an enjoyable visit for our guests."

He smiled graciously at them, all the while thinking of the deeds he had planned to convince them to leave. He gulped his drink and left.

Chapter 29

Captured.   Tahiti Noveau Hotel and Resort

Vicky sat alone in her room. Her earlier tryst with Claude was still vivid in her mind. She had never succumbed to her desires during any of her past misadventures. She tried to wipe her feelings of affection for him away, but found it impossible. She was faced with a dilemma. Her greed for the financial gain from the scheme versus the satisfaction of having him as a lover, and still having access through him to great wealth. She faced a precipice that divided her from love and greed. The wrong decision would determine her fate. It tormented her. In her mind, she tried to rationalize abandoning the scheme to collapse the de Passioné businesses. It seemed impossible. There were too many others with vested interests who would seek retaliation. The bloodthirsty Chinese gang with their aspirations to turn the company laboratories into facilities to produce fentanyl and other synthetic drugs and disguise them using advanced techniques. They had already mastered a technique to disguise cocaine from detection by mixing it in suspension in new bottles of wine. They had devised an extraction process that recovered the cocaine without any adverse effects. Research was underway for the same process with fentanyl. The Chinese had invested in the scheme and would not be easily convinced to walk away.

Vicky continued exploring options to cancel the project. It seemed impossible. Luigi Fratti in Italy had forged a strong relationship with the Chinese, for them to supplement his drug supplies from Colombia. The Colombian link was becoming less reliable due to the intercepts and detection from the US and other countries. He needed the Chinese to produce the drugs at de Passioné facilities in France using undetectable methods. She could not rely on Luigi to agree and stop the project.

It seemed hopeless. She considered whether influencing Sir Reginald and Arnie Jacobson to kill the financial maneuvers would doom the project. She quickly gave up on that idea, as the financial returns for them were huge, and neither would forego that.

Sitting alone and realizing the impossibility of extracting herself from the plan, she became depressed. Quietly, she cursed at her stupidity for allowing herself to get into a romantic situation with Claude. Her role was to simply abduct him and make him disappear while the financial games were played, and suppliers to de Passioné were paid off to sabotage the supply of critical materials. She had failed.

Her melancholy mood was shattered by the vibrating of her secure satellite phone. She immediately knew something of importance had happened. Only Sir Reginald and Luigi Fratti had access to the number for the phone and the corresponding equipment needed to access her phone. Gingerly, she answered, wondering what crisis had unfolded.

She clicked on the 'Establish Link' button and waited. Sir Reginald's crisp, accented British voice announced his presence on the link.

"Vixen, we may have a big problem. I received a detailed call and some video from Knuckles O'Brien. You have an unwelcome visitor there in Tahiti. He reports that Barry Jones, Claude's confidant and right-hand man, has arrived there. Knuckles has had him under surveillance since his arrival. He has been visiting different hotels and restaurants and asking questions. 'Knuckles' reports that Barry Jones has provided employees at those establishments with financial incentives to report any clues or information on Claude's whereabouts to him. It seems you were careless and said too much at a restaurant. The employee confirmed to Knuckles that it was Claude who was there. I am sure you are well aware of the consequences that will await you if you blow this operation. Now, get yourself together and go to ground with him. Contact the people at the number I gave you. Do it immediately."

Vicky panicked. She had suspected the cover was blown because of Claude's behavior at the restaurant, and later, when she had seen 'Knuckles' watching them from a distance. She listened as the link dropped and the inactive link tone sounded. It was clear that a wrong move now could result in the end of her life.

She was trapped and needed to decide between saving Claude and the business, or ignoring her emotions and pushing ahead with the original plan. Either was fraught with severe consequences. She dialed the number that had been provided to her and was advised that a car would come for her.

Her thoughts were interrupted by a loud knock at the door. Cautiously, she called out requesting the identity of the person.

"It's Henri from the Front Desk. The hotel wishes to send you a complimentary gift, and I am here to deliver it."

"It is inconvenient for me to answer the door as I have changed into my nightgown. Please leave it at the door."

"I cannot do that, madam. My instructions are to hand it to you directly."

Vicky sensed a problem.

"Alright, please take it back to the reception desk, and I will pick it up later."

Silence.

A full minute passed.

"OK. I will take it to the desk. A man stopped at my desk and asked for your room number. He says it is for a surprise visit to you and the other man with you. Should I provide the number to him?"

"I am not expecting anyone, and I am here alone. There is no man with me. Check the register, and if you have doubts, I am sure housekeeping will be able to tell you if another person is using this room with me. Now I must go to sleep. I will stop at the desk in the morning."

"My supervisor will not be pleased when I return with your gift."

"I am sorry about that. Now, goodnight."

Vicky waited fifteen minutes before running to Claude's room. She banged on the door. Claude answered with a huge smile when he recognized it was her.

"I received an urgent call. There is an emergency. I need to go to an associate's home here immediately. I will probably never return to this hotel. I am scared. Will you come with me?"

"What happened?"

"It is complicated. I will explain on the way there."

"Of course, I will accompany you. Do I need to bring anything?"

"No, as I am sure you will want to come back here and finish your vacation. I will leave my things here in case I can return. Let us go. I cannot delay."

Claude turned and walked back into his room and slipped on a pair of casual loafers.

"Ok, let's go."

Vicky draped her arm through his to give anyone watching the impression they were a couple strolling to the bar or hotel restaurant. She needed to keep their departure low profile.

She lowered her head as they passed by the reception area and exited the hotel. A dark, nondescript Ford was waiting outside the doors. She signaled the car, and it pulled forward.

"Don't worry. My associates sent this car for me. They will take me to their home so I can assist with the problem. It seems a key person has created a major problem that will financially impact our investment portfolio tomorrow when the exchange opens. "

"But surely there are others at your firm who can deal with this."

"No, I am in charge of the complete fund."

"But I don't understand. Why won't you be able to return to the hotel? This is strange."

"You will understand when we get there and it is all explained." They drove on in silence. The driver and his companion remained quiet.

Claude looked at them. They hardly seemed to fit the image of financiers. They looked like gangsters. He was getting concerned.

They continued to drive away from the coast and the hotel area into a residential area. The roads were dirt and unpaved, and the houses were basic and in poor repair. The driver turned sharply, and they started to drive up an incline beneath a rugged, low mountain. After several minutes, the driver turned into an overgrown driveway that led to a single-story house. The house was hidden from view by a dense growth of trees and shrubs. Instead of stopping at the front of the house, the driver continued down a path to a small building at the rear of the house. He stopped the car and turned to Vicky.

"We are here at the office, Miss. I will assist you and help you into the office."

Silent alarm bells sounded in Claude's head.

The driver took Claude's arm and guided him through the door. Inside, another man grabbed Claude's other arm while a sickly thin man approached a jabbed a large hypodermic syringe into Claude's neck. Within a minute, Claude crumpled to the floor.

The sickly man turned to Vicky and, through his yellowed and crooked teeth, snarled at her.

"Lucky it's not you, Princess. Mind you, if it were I'd have some fun with that body of yours while you were sleeping."

"Antoine, you are a pig."

"Careful there Princess, as the boss tells me you fucked up and for me to take care of you. I am just the man to do that."

"You touch me and you will regret it."

"Let's not get distracted. The priority is to get your friend away from Tahiti. The boss tells me there is a problem. Someone has come looking for him. He will not be leaving here until we have arrangements in place to get him off the island. I have been instructed to eradicate you both if things do not go as planned. I hope I am clear. So, go ahead and make yourself at home. You will be confined here until we arrange to move him from the island."

"You are an idiot. My possessions are at the hotel as well as his. It will only be a matter of time before our absence is noticed, and then the hotel security will call in the police and other authorities, who will find my sat phone and the drugs used on him during the abduction. In addition, they will find his papers, including identification. You are making a huge mistake by keeping me here."

"No, not at all. You seem to overlook that we have our people working at the hotel. They will be contacted to remove all the articles from your rooms. The hotel will be advised that you both have to leave due to business reasons, and we will settle the accounts. That will not raise any suspicions. I am sure you now realize you are not in control. You are in a very weak position. Your involvement is no longer important, so it doesn't matter if you were to die. It will only leave more to be shared amongst us."

The reality hit Vicky hard. She had been manipulated into this situation. Angrily, she determined to escape and seek out those who betrayed her with a vengeance.

Her captor sneered at her and left the room, locking the steel door behind him. Vicky examined the room. It was a well-disguised cell. A small toilet was in the corner. High windows glazed with bulletproof Lexan allowed in dim light but prevented any escape as they were resistant to breakage. She was captured in a cell that was more secure than most jail cells.

Vicky sat down on the dirty mattress of the truckle bed to consider her options, which seemed to be few. She looked at the crumpled heap of Claude lying on the cement floor where they had left him.

Despair flooded through her. She had trusted the wrong people.

Chapter 30

de Passion residence, France

Buzz had woken early. He had placed calls to Barry and was concerned when he could not contact him. Today was the day he planned to provide Sir Reginald and Lady Agnes with an experience they would never forget.

Last night, while the others were enjoying their cognacs, he had slipped away to speak with the head vintner who had requested a meeting. At the meeting, he was informed that Sir Reginald had been asking questions of the employees and had offered money for several to keep him informed about the problems caused by the disruption of supplies, and asked what else would cause delays and problems. Sir Reginald requested a copy of certain financial documents. He offered more money for them. The men advised him that they would need to get the information overnight, and he could get it in the morning. They intended to use the delay to produce false numbers. The employees were loyal to the de Passioné family. They had always been treated well and refused to be involved. Buzz was furious when he learned of the interference by Sir Reginald. He spoke with the employees, and together they hatched a plan that Buzz was sure would terrify the guests and send them packing.

Buzz was convinced that Sir Reginald was one of the instigators of the problems that the de Passioné businesses were presently experiencing, but needed proof. He had contacted former law officials with whom he had worked in his previous career. He intended to stop whoever and whatever was designed to hurt the de Passioné family and business.

Buzz tried to call Barry again without success. He wanted to forewarn him of the planned event, as he was sure Marie-France would panic. He did not want her to get Barry involved unnecessarily.

He looked out at the early dawn breaking. There had been fresh snow overnight. The sky was clear and looked cold. Buzz considered it the ideal condition for his planned 'crisis'.

He was snapped out of his thoughts by the sounds of movement from the kitchen, as the staff arrived and set about preparing breakfast. He smiled, thinking Sir Reginald and Lady Agnes would need a good breakfast before encountering the adventure he and some of the staff had planned.

There was a shuffling sound, and Buzz turned to see Sir Reginald at the door dressed in a heavy coat and wearing a beret.

"Good morning, Buzz. I like to take a little walk before breakfast. I will be back soon."

Buzz was thrilled he was going out. It allowed him time to doctor the food. He went into the kitchen and addressed the staff.

"Please make a pot of tea for our guests and a pot of coffee for me and Marie-France. Call me when the tea is ready. The guest is walking, so wait a few minutes before preparing it. Let me know, and I will take it to them."

He returned to the salon to find Lady Agnes and Marie-France.

"Good morning, ladies. Sir Reginald has gone for a short walk. He will be back in a few minutes, and we can all enjoy a nice breakfast. I have a special morning planned for you."

Lady Agnes beamed. She loved being the center of attention.

"Dress warmly as we will be out in the country."

Buzz walked across the room and looked from the window to see Sir Reginald heading into the winery office. He would soon be given the false information. Buzz was pleased with the way things were progressing.

As he watched, the office door opened and Sir Reginald reappeared. He was reaching inside his coat and inserting some papers into his coat pocket. Buzz smiled. Sir Reginald had taken the bait.

"I can see him approaching the house. I will go and tell the kitchen staff to be ready with breakfast."

Sir Reginald returned and informed them he would join them after changing to lighter clothing. Buzz couldn't believe his luck. He needed the time to 'prepare' the tea.

A servant entered the salon carrying a tray of fresh croissants, butter, and jams. She set them down on the table and announced she would return with the coffee and cream. Buzz jumped up from his chair.

"I will come with you to the kitchen and bring in the fresh tea for Lady Agnes."

In the kitchen, Buzz opened the lid of the teapot and poured in a large dose of Dulcolax Saline Liquid. The invisible tasteless laxative was sure to work an hour or so after they ate. Buzz smiled at the thought and took the tea back into the salon.

When Sir Reginald joined them, Buzz passed around the pastries and poured tea for them, making sure that Marie-France received coffee and not tea. Eager to get the guests out of the house, Buzz steered the conversation.

"I suggest I drive you up to see the latest vineyard we acquired. We will pass through some beautiful farmland on the way. I will need to handle a little business, and then we can visit the little restaurant in the village for an early lunch. Maybe after that, Marie-France can join us in the village to visit those quaint stores."

"That sounds splendid."

"Wrap up and let's go. The best time to see the countryside is early in the morning. You are both in for a treat."

Minutes later, they piled into the estate's Land Rover and started on their adventure. The country road was wet with melting snow. After a while, it was no longer sealed and became a dirt road. The Land Rover bucked and lurched along the uneven surface, at times sliding to the edge of the slippery mud. Buzz smiled in anticipation of meeting the men he had convinced to assist him with an 'incident.'

The Land Rover labored up a steep incline and occasionally lost traction and slipped back. Each time, Lady Agnes would emit a little yelp. Ahead, Buzz spied the three men he had hired to help with the 'problem'. He deliberately steered the vehicle into the soft mud at the edge. The Land Rover immediately sank into the mud.

Buzz cursed and went through the theatrics of attempting the steer out of the mud. He hoped Sir Reginald had not seen him disengage all-wheel drive.

The wheels spun, and the vehicle rocked forward but remained stuck. The three men approached. Each was carrying a rifle and looked particularly menacing.

The tallest man knocked on the driver's window. Buzz lowered the window, and the man called to him. Sir Reginald and Lady Agnes were unable to decipher the rapidly spoken French. The man summoned his partners, and they walked to the back of the Land Rover to try pushing the vehicle. As they walked past, one of the men leered at Lady Agnes and gave her a wink and toothiest smile. She was horrified.

Buzz dropped the Land Rover into gear and gently accelerated. There was no movement. The man returned to Buzz and shouted as he pointed to the passengers.

"He wants you to get out and help. He thinks your weight inside is not helping."

They squeezed out of the Land Rover and onto the muddy surface. Sir Reginald assisted Lady Agnes to the rear of the vehicle. The three men took a position on either side. When they indicated they were ready, Buzz engaged the gears and accelerated again. Mud and gravel flew as the rear wheels spun, coating both Lady Agnes and Sir Reginald with cold, wet mud. Sir Reginald continued to push with all his strength, and the vehicle lurched forward. As it did, his stomach reacted to the strain and exertion. His bowels exploded, and the laxative encouraged excrement sprayed. A sickly stench filled the immediate air. The three men quickly moved away and stared at Sir Reginald aghast. Sir Reginald stood dripping mud and oozing excrement from his fashionable country squire outfit. He was about to speak when Lady Agnes called to him. She was also caked in mud, but was holding her stomach and bent over. A look at her feet and the ground around her indicated the laxative had done its job. A high-pitched wail emanated from her as she started to weep.

Buzz jumped out and walked to the rear to view the scene. He wanted to laugh, but remained composed.

"This is not so good. Well, at least we got the vehicle unstuck."

He assisted them into the cargo area at the back of the Land Rover.

"Get in there. We can hose that out when we get back to the winery. No harm done. Now, should we carry on so you can see our latest purchase?"

Lady Agnes exploded; her ladylike mannerisms were gone.

"No. Get me home. I want to leave this barbaric country. Those horrible men. Reginald, did you see what he did? I don't feel safe. I am a mess. How can I ever get that mess of me? The smell is atrocious. Buzz, drive faster. I want to leave this place and get home to Britain today. At least we have decent people with manners and food that doesn't make you ill. This is a horrible country."

Buzz drove on in silence. The Land Rover rocked and twisted along the dirt road. It was too much for Sir Reginald. Buzz heard the moan and looked in the rear vision mirror to witness Sir Reginald vomiting. There was shouting as his vomit landed on Lady Agnes.

Buzz chuckled. "This couldn't have gone better," he thought.

They arrived back at the residence, and Buzz slowed down.

"I don't think you should go into the residence like that. I will drive you to the vineyard workshop. There we have a fully equipped shower area. You can shower and clean off. There are no workers there today, so you will be fine. After your showers, there are clean coveralls and boots you can wear until we get you to the residence."

"I am indignant. How can you imagine expecting a lady like me to shower in some workers' bathroom? God knows what germs are in there or what disease I will catch. I am not having it."

Buzz listened to her tirade. He was sick of her.

"Lady Agnes. The facility is fine. It is better than some found at private clubs or sports facilities. You must clean off before entering the residence."

"I will not. At least, not in a workers' bathroom."

"Have it your way, but you will not go into the residence like that. I have another solution. Get out and stand by the gate. Let me get the high-pressure hose and wash you."

Lady Agnes became apoplectic.

In the rear, Sir Reginald was dry heaving. He looked like death and smelled like a sewer.

Finally, Lady Agnes and a stumbling Sir Reginald accepted their fate and walked into the showers.

"Throw your clothes outside in the bin. We have a commercial laundry to clean the men's clothing. I will have yours done and packed."

Lady Agnes was indignant.

"I will never wear those clothes again. Throw them out."

Buzz left them to find some clean coveralls and boots.

Showered, Buzz assisted them onto the back seat of the Land Rover for the short ride to the residence. Lady Agnes was still furious and swearing.

Buzz stopped at the front stairs and waited for them to leave the Land Rover. He watched as they climbed the stairs, looking like a couple of white mummified corpses.

They were met at the door by Marie-France, who was shocked at their appearance.

"What happened? Why are you dressed like that?"

Lady Agnes turned to her and swore.

"Don't fucking speak to me. I am leaving this dump immediately."

"What happened?"

"Your idiot husband got us stuck in the mud. Some rough farmhands came to help. One almost raped me. Now, out of my way. I am getting dressed in real clothes and arranging a flight back to London."

The words stung. Marie-France stood dumbfounded as Lady Agnes stormed off. Marie-France turned and looked at Buzz for answers.

"It is best they leave. I will explain it all later when they have gone. Do not be upset."

"It troubles me that a family member is leaving our home under unpleasant circumstances."

"When I explain it, then you will understand. It is for the best."

In the distance, Buzz could hear the phone in the small office area ring. He left to answer it. It was Barry. Buzz relayed to Barry the morning's drama and heard Barry howling with laughter.

"I am meeting someone who should be able to assist us this evening. So far, I have nothing to report. We only know that Claude's credit card was used, and the waiter at a restaurant has confirmed it was Claude who dined there. I will be in contact when there is something to report."

A servant knocked at the door of the office and handed Buzz an envelope. It was from Horatio Henderson. He read the note.

Buzz. I have taken an unplanned and quick trip to New York. Our forensics team, headed by Sylvia Piper, has made a discovery that may be significant. I need to discuss and obtain the assistance of others here in New York. I will return as soon as possible. I will not go into detail now until we have proof and can confirm details.

Horatio.

Buzz wondered what had been discovered to be so important that Horatio left for New York.

He returned to find Sir Reginald and Lady Agnes standing at the entrance, waiting for a taxi to take them to the airport. He turned and walked away from them. Marie-France stood embarrassed and attempted to placate them. It was no use. Lady Agnes stared at her coldly.

"I don't know why you live in these conditions with such horrible people. Shame on you. Don't bother contacting me again. You are not family."

Tears welled in Marie-France's eyes as they hurriedly rushed out to the waiting taxi.

Buzz stood beside her as they watched the taxi pull away.

"I think that one day you and Claude will thank me."

Chapter 31

The Chinese Factor

In Guangdong Province, China, Lee Chang walked through the streets of the small village. He had escaped the authorities' purge of the many families who had been boiling and making methamphetamine. Hundreds had been arrested, and some were executed as the authorities attempted to shut down the businesses.

He walked past many of the old deserted houses surrounded by piles of bricks, broken sticks, household garbage, and knee-high weeds. Many of the villagers had fled in search of safer places to live and hide away from the ever-present police and gangs of lawless young men.

As he walked, he looked up at several expensive houses located amongst the rubble and decay of what once had been a thriving fishing village, before the arrival of the drug trade. The fishermen had abandoned their boats and an income of a few hundred yuan a month for the riches associated with selling the meth or the ingredients need to manufacture it. Others who were not making the drug were earning large sums by smuggling in the chemicals needed in the manufacturing process in their boats. Those expensive houses he knew belonged to his fellow criminals or the crooked party leaders.

Lee Chang's interests had graduated from lowly meth to the more lucrative and in-demand business of fentanyl production. His problem was the difficulty in producing the product. The primitive methods used to manufacture meth or the compounds used in its production were useless. Through his extensive underworld connections, he had established a strong relationship with Luigi Fratti and the Italian drug distribution network he operated.

He had met Luigi in Europe at a late-night drinking party and had lamented how it was difficult to manufacture fentanyl in China, as the corrupt cops would inform the authorities. If the payoff was not large, their 'security personnel' would visit, and the operation would be smashed. While Lee Chang was a powerful gang leader, the corrupt police and local politicians were able to disrupt his activities. It made his ability to offer a consistent supply of the drug to his dealers impossible. In addition, the police and politicians were taking larger cuts of the profits.

Luigi spent days meeting with Lee Chang, and they eventually developed a friendship. Lee Chang returned to China with a new friend and a contact to further sell his drugs. He was happy.

Months later, Lee Chang received a mysterious message from Luigi asking if they could meet. Luigi suggested the meeting take place in France, and a date and place were established.

Weeks passed until they finally met at the Grand Hotel de l'Opéra in Toulouse. Lee Chang was accompanied by two large and fierce-looking Chinese bodyguards. Other patrons of the hotel looked at them with obvious fear.

Over the next few days, Luigi spent time with Lee Chang ascertaining whether he could trust him enough to bring him into the plan regarding the de Passioné project.

"Lee Chang, I have some very serious business I wish to discuss with you. I suggest we have dinner alone. Do not bring your men. We must be seen as a couple of businessmen having a quiet, friendly dinner, not a meeting that requires guards that could draw attention. "

Lee started to object, but curiosity won out, and he agreed.

"Tonight at 7, I will meet you at the 'Oiseau Bleu' restaurant. It is very private and we will be able to speak without others eavesdropping. I will request a private booth."

Luigi considered the risk of involving the Chinese gang. He decided a second opinion was needed. He placed a call the Arnie Jacobson in New York.

"Arnie, an opportunity has presented itself. It will benefit us financially, and there will be an added benefit. As with all opportunities in my business, there is a risk, and I would like to discuss this with you."

Luigi outlined the possibility of including Lee Chang and his operation. He stressed the need to find a European supplier for the fentanyl. Intercepts and seizures of the drug by the authorities had increased, and the losses were significant. A supplier was needed who would not be subjected to searches at the borders. Luigi highlighted the use of the laboratories of the de Passioné wineries for testing the wines and spirits. He proposed to Arnie to establish a secure facility to produce fentanyl and other synthetic drugs under the guise of a legitimate laboratory.

Arnie Jacobson listened but remained uncommitted.

"What business arrangement do you propose? The Chinese are bloodthirsty and untrustworthy. I am not comfortable with what you suggest. How can you control them? The Chinese are indeed very astute when money is involved, but they will look after their interests at the expense of others. How would we gain financially from an arrangement such as this?"

"We will retain ownership of the labs. They will pay us a percentage of the revenue from the sale of the drugs. The costs to set up the labs will not be large. The Chinese already own much of the equipment needed to make the products. We can arrange to ship it here."

"A system will need to be established to handle the movement of funds. With the governments of most countries monitoring transfers to supposedly prevent laundering for terrorist groups and such, it has become a little more difficult. My company does have a Chinese trading fund established. It has been operating for years and assists with investment banking for both US and Chinese companies. It could handle certain transactions between China and Europe. I am interested, but there will be conditions."

"Lee Chang has been involved in drug trafficking for years. He established sophisticated networks between Colombia and Europe using the Caribbean islands as transit points. While he loses a portion of the shipments to the actions of the US Coast Guard and DEA, he can satisfy his customers in North America and Europe. His people have devised clever ways to disguise the shipments. They perfected a method to ship cocaine by dissolving it in drinks and cosmetics. A method to extract the cocaine was devised and worked perfectly. I intend to ask his people to research doing the same with fentanyl, but using wine. That way, we can use the wine produced at de Passioné to transport the drug."

"If that can be done, that is genius, and I will certainly invest. Yes, I think you should proceed with the Chinese."

Satisfied that Arnie Jacobson was onboard, Luigi contacted Lee Chang to confirm the meeting.

Later that evening, Luigi met Lee Chang at the Grand Hotel de l'Opéra. Over the meal, Luigi described the plan to manipulate and take over the de Passioné vineyards and wineries. Lee Chang's interest was piqued.

"Luigi, this is an outstanding idea. There are also benefits to me that I am sure you have not realized. In China, the interest and consumption of wines have increased dramatically over the past 10 years. Not only can we manufacture the drugs, but we can also operate the business and export to China and the rest of the world. It is brilliant."

"The financial transactions will be handled through our partners in London and New York. That is not negotiable."

"I have many questions. Who are the other partners? I will not invest if there are any of my competitors or enemies are involved. I need to meet with them all before we commit."

"That can be arranged. I suggest we call a meeting to be held in London."

"Yes, that will be easier. I will need to include my senior adviser. He has been involved in my business for many years and is most trusted."

"Before I can agree to that, you will need to disclose who that is. I will need to inform the others. It will only happen if all partners agree. Now, I must ask you to keep this confidential. I await your decision to advise us of who this partner is. After the partners agree, we will meet. I advise you that the plan is moving ahead very quickly, and already some steps have been taken. You may be aware of the disappearance of Claude de Passioné. He has been abducted by us. We intend to use him to guarantee success with the takeover."

"I will return to China tomorrow. You will have the information in a few days."

Chapter 32

Papeete. Offices of DGSE.French Intelligence

Denis Ricard welcomed Barry and introduced Colonel Pierre Leclair, the Head of DGSE, the Directorate-General of External Security.

"I welcome you, but wish it were in circumstances better than these. Denis has briefed me on the situation. It is very disturbing. Our organization, DGSE, is part of our fine French Military and has the mandate to protect French interests internationally. The de Passioné businesses are a special part of French history and Culture, with influence in international markets. I understand from Denis that forces external to France are involved. Please take your time and brief me on everything. If I know the extent of what is happening, I will be able to advise and, hopefully, assist. But first, let me have some coffee and pastries delivered, as I think this is going to take some time."

Barry sat back and started to describe how events at the wineries affected production. He detailed the historical relationships with vendors, customers, and Investment Banks.

Colonel Leclair listened without interrupting.

An hour passed before Barry completed his delivery.

"What you tell me is most disturbing. In summary, it appears that both France's international interests and our internal security are threatened. I think we need to involve our sister organization, DGSI. They handle matters of internal security. We can work together in a situation like this. I will summon my counterpart."

Colonel Leclair excused himself and left to arrange for the Head of DGSI to join them. It took a while, but a tall hawkish man returned with the Colonel.

"Let me introduce Monsieur Marc Poirier, Head of DGSI."

Introductions were made, and the Colonel described the threat.

"I understand that Claude de Passioné is missing, and there is evidence he is here in Papeete. Do you think he is here alone and voluntarily, or is it possible he has been abducted?"

"I have known Claude for many years. He has had bad times in the past that many would have had problems handling. Claude is strong. I believe he intended to take a short time here after his marriage breakup in Rarotonga, but it is unlike him to stop communicating. I have been his confidant through many bad situations. I believe he is in some sort of trouble."

Silence filled the room before Marc Poirier spoke.

" I will assign my best men to liaise with the local police. We should have an accurate description of recent activities and the characters involved in local crime. The island is small enough that it is relatively easy to keep track of the criminals. Something like the abduction of Claude will get leaked. The criminals here are not too smart. The majority of crime here is domestic assault, car theft, break-ins, tourist theft, drunkenness, and on occasion, the odd murder. Something like an abduction of a foreign executive would be major for them, and only a few gangs would be able to handle it. We should have some information soon."

Barry was relieved to hear Marc Poirier's assessment. Marc Poirier excused himself and left for another meeting.

They left the meeting room, and Denis suggested a working lunch at a nearby restaurant. Barry was surprised to see Fleur Leclair in the office lobby.

"Fleur, what are you doing here? When did you arrive here?"

"I heard you were coming to meet my father, and I wanted to see you and my father. As a family member of a high-ranking officer, I am entitled to fly on a government plane, and there was one leaving not long after leaving San Francisco. So here I am."

"It is nice to see you, but as I mentioned, I am a married man."

"No, my interest is not romantic. I know many people and may be able to assist you in finding your Claude. I grew up here and know some of the people who might be suspects. They were friends when we were younger. They will talk to me, but not the police. I want to help."

"But you have your life in San Francisco. What about your university studies?"

"I had a break from my studies and wanted to return home to see my parents and friends. You have given me a great excuse to be here."

Denis smiled as he looked at Barry.

"You must join us for lunch, my dear. It will be nice to have something nice to chat about besides boring Barry."

"Oh, no. I can assure you, he is not boring. He is a handsome adventurer."

They walked from the offices to a nearby bistro. They were seated at the front beside a large window that opened onto the boulevard.

Without hesitation, and to demonstrate his appreciation of fine wines, Denis ordered them all a drink. Barry was impressed by the selection.

For a while, they sat talking and joking. Barry excused himself to visit the toilet. As he walked through the dining area, he noticed a bearded man with strange brown hair. He was sure it was the same man he had seen in the hotel lobby that morning, but did not think much about the coincidence.

At the table, the waiter was making a production of describing the menu items. Barry smiled as he recognized that the waiter was trying to impress Fleur. He sat and continued sipping his wine. The conversation continued with Fleur telling Denis of her life growing up in Tahiti. Barry looked up in the direction of the bearded man and was surprised to see him staring directly at him. He was sure he was being watched. He stood and made the excuse of needing a medicine he had forgotten, but needed to take when he ate.

"I saw a store. I will be back in a minute."

Barry walked slowly along the street. It was busy with workers out for lunch. He looked into store windows to see the reflection behind him. At the street corner, he saw the man. He was being followed. Barry turned and quickly walked to rejoin the others. They were eating lunch when Barry noticed the man re-enter the bistro. He decided to find out who the man was and why he was being followed. He leaned over the table to Denis.

"Denis, don't look now, but I have a man tailing me. He was at the hotel this morning, and now I see him here at lunch. He was staring directly at me. When I left to go to the store, he followed, and now he is back here. I intend to find out who he is."

"No. Do not do that. Fleur, can you go back to the office and advise the Colonel? He can have people from DGSI join us for lunch, and they can ascertain the situation. They are better equipped and have access to information you don't. If he is following you, there are several reasons I can think of. He may be following you if he believes you know where Claude is. It is also possible that he is working with others who may have taken Claude. Are you sure he is following you?"

"Denis, from the way he is dressed, he just doesn't fit in. He is not wearing the clothes of a tourist, nor is he dressed like a local worker here. His clothing is heavy, like British."

Denis casually turned and, while observing the man, signalled the waiter.

Fleur agreed to return and advise her father of the man's activities and request someone from DGSI to return to the restaurant with her. She left, and Denis ordered another bottle of wine.

"This will be a nice way to pass the time and not arouse his suspicions. It will give Fleur a chance to brief her father and return with someone qualified to investigate the individual."

Chapter 33

Tantamore Capital, London, England

Sir Reginald looked at the pile of correspondence on his desk. His short visit to France continued to annoy him. He did not receive the information he had hoped to obtain from the workers at the de Passioné winery. Lady Agnes had hysterically rejected his romantic overtures after their return. He could still smell the effluent and mud that had splattered them both. He was still suffering a stomach cramp, and the trip had tired him. He was not happy, and it showed.

Annoyed at the outcome of the trip, he was determined to accelerate the plan. His patience had run out, plus he had allocated millions of pounds to acquire and manipulate the share values of the de Pasioné companies.

He sat alone in his office reviewing the results they had achieved so far. The financial strength of the de Passioné businesses had been weakened, the bankers were nervous and eager to cooperate in collapsing the companies and retrieving what capital they could. Claude de Passioné was now safely captured, Arnie Jacobson was ready to move, and Luigi Fratti was willing to participate. All was ready. His thought wandered to Vicky Spagnoli. He decided she was now expendable, even though the idea of taking control of the de Passioné empire had been hers and she had developed the plan. She had outlived her usefulness. He was disappointed she had not controlled Claude's capture better. The stupid move of allowing Claude exposure and the use of his credit card put everything at risk. He decided he was done with her. She was finished.

Feeling the thrill before the action, Sir Reginald requested a cup of tea to enjoy before he called Arnie Jacobson and started the first event to bring down de Passioné.

He looked at the time. Late afternoon in the UK. With the time difference to the East Coast US, the New York Exchanges would be closed. The timing was ideal. He was not worried about the US West Coast brokers, as they did not have enough influence to interfere financially.

In the quiet of his office and while sipping his tea, Sir Reginald ran the intended sequence of actions through his mind. It was the day he had been waiting for. He considered retirement after this one final act.

He was snapped out of his vision by the buzzing of his satellite phone. Before answering, he wondered whether it was Vicky or Arnie. He hoped it was not Vicky.

He answered the phone. It was neither Vicky nor Arnie Jacobson, it was Knuckles O'Brien. In a thick Irish Brogue, Knuckles delivered the news.

"Governor, we've got quite the pickle here. Barry Jones has arrived. He is talking with the French DGSI. Those boyos don't fuck around. Jesus, mighty, these lads are the ones who stop the terrorists. Those bandits holding your Claude boy don't stand a fuckin chance against them You've got to get Claude off the island immediately if you want your little game to go ahead and be successful."

Sir Reginald was well aware of the DGSI. He cursed. He had not expected Barry Jones to go looking for Claude, but now with the DGSI involved, the game had changed. He could deal with Vicky, but he needed Claude alive, as he was the key component in implementing the final step of the plan. They had intended to kidnap Marie-France as ransom. Claude was to sign over all control and ownership of the de Passioné holdings. He was more than prepared to give the order to execute Marie-France if Claude did not comply. After the disastrous trip he had just been on, giving that order would be a pleasure.

If she were executed, however, and the business was not signed over, the plan called for the execution of Claude as well. All the partners had agreed that killing Claude was a last resort, as the business would fail and close. They wanted it as an operating business.

The fact that Barry Jones had arrived was bad enough, but to have the DGSI involved was a disaster. He worried that Knuckles O'Brien would panic. He needed him there to monitor the situation.

"Do not do anything until I contact you. I need to speak with others."

"I am going to keep following Barry Jones. If he gets help from the DGSI to look for your man, I will know and report."

After Knuckles hung up, Sir Reginald recalled his last discussion with Vicky. He had sensed a change in her but was unsure why. He wondered whether to call her and update her on the developments. He decided against any action until after he had spoken to Arnie Jacobson. He had not foreseen the problems with capturing Claude. Now there was a big problem.

He waited impatiently until Arnie answered his private secure line.

"Reginald. Great that you called. I was about to call you."

"So you have heard. We have problems."

"What are you talking about? I was calling to discuss a meeting I had with Luigi. What problem?"

Sir Reginald filled Arnie in with all the details. When finished, Arnie let out a long whistle.

"Reginald, you have a big issue. To be accurate, you now have two big issues."

Arnie told Reginald of the call with Luigi and his bringing Lee Chang into the group. Reginald was not happy and voiced his concern.

"Arnie, surely you remember the financing of the Chinese joint government and private investor program. The stated objectives were the development of the infrastructure and the financing of those regional projects. The only ones who won were the crooked politicians and the well-disguised gangs. We lost everything. It almost caused the collapse of my firm when the UK and US governments withdrew funds and demanded that we cancel certain investment programs. You will recall we had no help from the Chinese. Now you want to include some of the worst-known Chinese criminals in all of Asia. They will take over and we will be out."

"Reginald, bear in mind that you and I are only manipulating certain securities to our advantage. After the transaction is complete, we will not be involved. We have no interest in remaining invested in an operating wine business. That will be Luigi's problem. We will be long gone. Now, what is it you want to discuss? You previously told me a little, but I think there is a lot more."

"I have made a decision. Vicky has become a liability. She has not managed the confinement of Claude. Now we have a local gang in Tahiti involved. We needed them to lock up Claude at a secure location. I have Knuckles O'Brien on the ground there, but I am not convinced about him. Typically Irish. Offer him some cash and a whiskey, and he is yours. We are exposed. Without control of Claude, we will be in a weak position. We need to silence Vicky and get Claude out of Tahiti. I had considered asking Luigi for assistance, but remembered he had a long-term friendship with Vicky. I doubt he would help, and he may tip her off. If we make it sweet enough, I am sure Knuckles could be bought. We will need to dispose of him as well after the de Passioné deal is complete."

Arnie remained quiet. He considered the options, including using his people.

"Reggie, I think I have the solution. You have just solved the problem. We tell Lee Chang that the fee to join us is for him to get Claude safely away from Tahiti. I am sure his people will be happy to deal with Vicky, for a price."

Sir Reginald Coxburn did not respond immediately. He thought of the many times she had catered to his every whim. The idea of annihilating her seemed too severe. He wondered if he could control her. She was smart and always had his best interests at heart.

"I will think about it. There may be other solutions. We will talk tomorrow."

Chapter 34

de Passioné Estate, France

Buzz spent the early morning attending to mundane administrative matters. It was a late spring, and again, a light snow had dusted the fields and vineyard. The workers were eager to return to the vines and work outside. Until the weather changed and it warmed up, he needed to assign maintenance tasks. With the disruption to supplies, some work could not be undertaken. He had no option except to meet with the workers and explain the predicament. Buzz did not look forward to this. Things in France were in turmoil. Farmers were protesting recent legislation passed by the French government. There had been protests throughout the country. He feared that the prevailing mood amongst the farm owners and farmhands would extend into the de Passioné vineyards. Relations between the workers and the family had been excellent. Buzz hoped that would continue. The problems with suppliers, banks, and recently, the distributors, were barely manageable. Buzz hoped that Barry would be successful in his search for Claude, and soon the two of them would return.

His attention was interrupted by the ringing of his phone.

"Buzz, good morning. This is Horatio. Our forensics team here in New York has been digging into Sylvia Piper's findings, and indeed, there are some very unorthodox matters in the financial dealings amongst the investment bankers. Very worrisome. I assume there has not been any further progress made in locating Claude? Given what we have unearthed, it is even more important that we make serious decisions about how to continue the company's operations. Technically, given how certain documents have been forged, the business could be bankrupted by the actions of a few. The company does not meet the financial conditions established when financing was done to acquire Mondial. This is serious. Do you think Marie-France can understand and make those decisions?"

"No. Marie-France has been absent from dealing with any of the business affairs since Claude assumed total control."

"Does Barry Jones have full signing authority as an officer of the company?"

"Barry is not here. He has gone to assist with the search for Claude in Tahiti."

"This is a huge problem. As the auditors for the company, we are required to report on matters such as this. It is a serious legal requirement. We do have some leeway as the next reporting period is still sixty days away."

"Can we bridge any financial shortfall? Can we employ Tantamore Capital to assist in the short term until Barry and Claude return?"

"That is the last thing I recommend, as it seems they have been party to the forgery of the documents. I am highly suspicious of them. Buzz, our findings are complex. We will need to meet and review them in person. Can you come to the US?"

"No. Things are not stable here. Let me speak to Barry. Maybe he will be able to travel."

"If what we have found is true, then it is likely that criminal charges will be laid by the different Security Commissions. This is not just a US issue but involves the UK, France, Italy, and Australia as the main countries affected. As principals, Claude, Barry, Marie-France, and possibly you, will all go on trial. We must start to address this problem now and take steps to correct it."

"Horatio, can you please explain to me what the audit reveals? Please try to make the explanation simple. I am not an accountant."

"Yes. Simply put, some liquidity tests are tied to formulas. These formulas are complex, but they measure the company assets, cash position, inventory, values of shares, and indebtedness. There are more factors, but those are the main ones. When the purchase of Mondial was completed, certain of the agreements with the company's lenders were updated. In the process, both Tantamore Capital and the US firm of Arnie Jacobson acted as lead advisers for the consortium of lenders, in this case, the investment banks. Months after the purchase, both Tantamore and Jacobson engaged in several trading transactions that diluted the value of the company and increased its liabilities. In addition, and contrary to the financing agreements, some debt has been sold to unknown investors. These transactions are suspect, and the identity of the parties is questionable, as our investigations led us into a maze of numbered and shell companies. We cannot trace who the real owners are. Interestingly, these investors are in countries such as Nigeria, Italy, Switzerland, the Grand Caymans, and other questionable tax locations. Our analysts suspect this is a deliberate and clever plan to orchestrate a takeover of the company. All the components are in place for these parties to manipulate the finances and weaken or collapse the business."

Buzz sat quietly, trying to absorb the enormity of the situation.

"Horatio, how could this happen? Surely there are safeguards and monitoring systems to prevent this type of thing from happening."

"Buzz, while it isn't simple to achieve, it is possible. It only takes a few corrupt officials in the Regulator departments of the Security Commission. The majority of trades are handled by computerized systems, but these can be overridden. Both Tantamore and Jacobson may have people inside the system. That is the only way something like this could happen."

"Can you salvage things? Is it possible to correct things? Can the crooked trades be reversed?"

"It is a difficult process that will be hampered by the fact that there are multiple jurisdictions involved. Furthermore, there is nothing to prevent Tantamore or Jacobson from acting immediately, and with the documents they possess, it will be hard to challenge. Any effort to stall them would need to be fought in court, and that will take time, possibly years, and during that time the company will fail."

"What do you suggest?"

"Without Claude here, it will be difficult. I recommend that the lawyers for de Passioné be assembled for a briefing and to devise a plan to protect the family's private fortunes. Confidentiality is key. None of this must be leaked. We do not want to start any further concern or panic amongst the banks and investors. Our firm will explore the options to void those trades that Tantamore and Jacobson surreptitiously executed. I believe we can save the company and protect the family. It will be difficult and expensive."

"That bastard, Sir Reginald, was just here pretending to be visiting Marie-France on vacation. He was snooping and trying to find out things from the workers. I wish I had done a little more for him before he left."

"Buzz, has there been any progress made with the efforts to locate Claude?"

Buzz told Horatio the little he knew of the involvement of the French security operations, the DGSE, and the DGSI.

"Let us hope they can crack open the criminals and locate Claude. In my mind, this is all coordinated. They are planning to make their move soon."

Chapter 35

In captivity, Papeete, Tahiti

Vicky listened intently to the muffled voices she could hear in the outer room. Most were spoken in the local Polynesian dialect, and she had no idea of what was being discussed. The intensity of several of the voices led her to believe there was an argument. This was reinforced when she heard the slap and scuffle. Voices were raised. A gunshot terminated the argument.

Nervously, she looked down at the crumpled mass of Claude lying on the damp concrete floor. She had no idea of the time or how long he had lain there unconscious. She was worried for him, not knowing what drugs had been injected into him. He had not moved.

An unexpected gush of emotion hit her. She looked at Claude and began to question her original plan. She was angry with herself and annoyed that she had not spent more time researching the family. On paper, the de Passioné estates looked to be prime targets for a takeover. Vicky knew the players well, and with her financial position at Tantamore, she was well-versed in the methods used to manipulate the financial affairs of companies. Now she was not sure. During the time spent with Claude in close quarters, she had seen values and a side of him no one had ever spoken of. If she didn't know better, she wondered if she was falling in love with him. At that moment, Vicky decided on a scheme to save his life.

Vicky looked down at him closely and was surprised to see his lips in a partial smile. Even though he was drugged, he emanated a kind expression. There was no question in her mind. She had fallen for him. Now, a new conflict entered and tormented her mind. Was it worth abandoning for her greed for money, or should she continue with the plan?

She lowered herself onto the old truckle bed and was thinking of ways to escape when there was scraping at the door. A loud squeaking sound came from the door's rusted hinges. A shaft of light penetrated the dark room. Standing in the light was Knuckles O'Brien. She gasped.

Knuckles remained quiet until they were alone and the steel door closed and locked behind them.

"What are you doing here? Why are you here?"

"I have been here since you arrived in Tahiti. Sir Reginald had concerns about abducting Claude de Passioné. He does not trust you, and my job was to follow you and report to him. Recently, I have become aware of things that disturb me. I have lost trust, and you should as well. You are not in here locked up with Claude just to keep him company. Sir Reginald has taken steps to have you silenced. You are here as a prisoner. I was able to convince those gang members that I was here on behalf of Sir Reginald to confirm you had been captured and that Claude was still alive. You are in grave danger. There are others here in Tahiti that I know and who could help to save you, but right now, I am not sure who to trust. I need time to discover who I can trust."

"But why are you here? We are no friends."

"I am worried that Sir Reginald also has plans for me. I heard some disturbing things from others last night. It seems he has a project that is about to start, and he wants to clean up any loose ends. I am one of those loose ends. I am being replaced with members of a Chinese gang run by the ruthless Lee Chang. I do not hold any personal grudge against you, so I have decided that since I am in jeopardy, I may as well try to save you."

"How can you do that? Claude and I are locked up here and under guard."

"There are several of the gang here at present, and they are strong, but they are not smart. I will create a diversion once I can enlist some support. I will need a little time."

Knuckles looked down at the floor and Claude's twisted body.

"Is he OK?"

"I would feel better if he weren't on that floor. Will you help me lift him to the bed? If we escape from here, what will you do? I am sure Sir Reginald will act to find and kill us."

"I have some ideas. I will tell you later."

"But we are on an island. The only way off is by boat or air. We have access to neither, and the authorities will be looking for Claude."

"You do not know this, but Barry Jones has arrived here on the island. I intend to approach him."

At that news, Vicky perked up. She was aware of Barry and his reputation as a fearless and strong-willed individual. It gave her hope.

"Can we trust him?"

"It is a risk. If I need to, I will tell him of Sir Reginald and that he might be planning things against Claude, his family, and the business. From what I understand, Barry is very loyal to Claude and the family."

“Do you think this will work? Where will we go? I cannot return to England. Sir Reginald is thick with the gangs there. I wouldn’t survive a week.”

“I have an idea, I will discuss with Barry if he agrees to meet and be reasonable. I have a lot to trade with him, so he should be receptive to my ideas.”

“Will you return here? How will I know what is happening?”

“Yes. I will return as soon as I get some things done. In the meantime, don’t antagonize these people. They turn ugly very fast. Now I will go and talk to them. They are not too smart, so they will accept what I tell them.”

Knuckles banged his fist against the door. Minutes later, it was pushed open by the same sickly looking man. Knuckles addressed him.

“ She seems OK. Do not drug him anymore. We need to question him and get him to sign certain papers. He is no use to us if he cannot function. Sir Reginald will inflict punishment on all of you if he is injured or incapable of performing the tasks we require. I will be returning here with a partner the next day. Be ready and keep them well.”

Antoine looked at Knuckles and sneered.

“I’m going to need to speak to Sir Reggie about that. My orders are that only you are to be allowed in here. Unless he says it’s OK, you won't be bringing anybody in here.”

Knuckles smiled and walked past Antoine. He had a plan.

Chapter 36

Impatience

Each of the syndicate's members was impatient with the progress of the event. Each had concerns.

In his office in Calabria, Italy, Luigi Fratti paced the floor of his office. It had been many months since he had agreed to assist in financing Arnie Jacobson with the de Passioné deal. He had forwarded funds to offshore accounts and arranged payments to various underworld friends to negatively influence key suppliers to the de Passioné businesses. So far, there has been no financial return. He was growing tired of the interaction with Arnie and his British counterpart, Sir Reginald Coxburn. He regretted that he had not acted alone when Vicky had approached him with the plan. Instead, she had suggested using Sir Reginald and Tantamore Capital as the means to collapse the de Passioné family and their business. It sounded like a solid plan. He had excessive monies deposited in foreign banks that he was eager to move. Those funds were not productive. Based on Arnie's recommendation, he had worked with Sir Reginald to structure a system to move the money without it being detected. These funds would finance the collapse and allow him to attain ownership of the winery. He had dreamed of operating the winery as a legitimate business as a disguise for money laundering and drug trafficking. Things had changed since he had first agreed to his involvement in the plan. He had never agreed to the abduction of Claude, and now the Chinese were involved.

Luigi was worried. He wondered whether it was possible to call off the whole project. He sensed trouble ahead. The media was playing up the situation, and questions were being asked in certain quarters. If it were solely his decision, he would abandon the plan

and take his losses, but it was not just his decision. He would need to convince the one other person to whom he owed his existence, power, and financial status, but he was sure that person would not agree.
Luigi stopped pacing and sat at his desk with a glass of Chianti to think through his options.

In the Guangdong Province, China, Lee Chang sat in a conference with several ranking members of the police and ruling politicians for his area of operation. They were members of the dreaded Tong family gang.

The room was hot and smoke-filled. Two young Chinese girls attended to the men's requests for drinks and food. The atmosphere was heavy, as was the mood of the men.

Ming Hoe, the district mayor, spoke.

"I am speaking for the others here. We are concerned and not happy. We have been very patient, but no more. Our friends in the police have controlled the possibility of anyone disrupting our business. Lee Chang, we have made you very rich. You promised to include us in the French project. We like the idea of producing our products in France. It will make shipping and distribution so much easier. We are not happy about the progress. You made promises that were not kept. We have sent you money. Why are there problems?"

"I have explained to you all that there are other parties involved, and no one can act alone until Claude de Passioné is dealt with. I was informed today that Claude is being held captive by our people. You must be patient, as we are very close to the start of the action. Now is not the time to panic or act foolishly."

"Lee Chang, we have been patient. We accepted the words you spoke. You have not delivered. Please leave so we can speak as a group. We will inform you of our decision. Wait outside."

Ming Hoe waved one of the girls to escort Lee Chang from the room.

Spring weather had graced London. The blue skies and warm temperature assisted in placating Sir Reginald's mood. Patience was not a virtue he possessed. Since his return from the disastrous trip to France, his mind had been preoccupied with triggering the events to commence the process to collapse of the de Passioné businesses. He had grown frustrated with Arnie Jacobson, who was making decisions without consulting him. He despised the Americans' arrogance. Besides his reactions to Arnie Jacobson, the actions of Luigi were also an annoyance. He was unhappy that Luigi had brought Lee Chang in on the project. He was concerned as he had promised the Boss that he, Sir Reginald, would maintain control to the end. The Boss would not be happy with recent developments. While he had close relations with the Boss, all of the other members of the syndicate were unaware of the anonymous Boss. Even local gangs did not know of a more powerful presence than that of |Sir Reginald.

In New York, even though spring had arrived, a biting cold wind blew in off the Hudson River. Arnie Jacobson had left his office and strolled to his favorite Jewish deli for a pastrami on rye with a pickle and greasy fries. The cold wind penetrated his layers of clothing. Arnie decided he would escape the cold in Mexico after the deal was over.

As he walked, his mind played back the sequence of events that had led him to his involvement with Sir Reginald and the others. It had been Luigi who had introduced him. His relationship with Luigi spanned years and was established out of need. Luigi required a means to launder his illegally gained drug money, and

Arnie was only too happy to oblige for a fee. Arnie considered the other players and reassessed his risk. He could not identify a weak link and considered the plan safe.

Sir Reginald's comments about terminating Vicky worried him. He was aware of the strong bond between her and Luigi and was concerned that Luigi might disagree and try to stop it. That could lead to problems. He was impatient and wanted the matter done, considering that the longer the delay, the greater the likelihood of failure. He did not want to be caught in a situation like that.

Tired of Sir Reginald's continued excuses and delays, Arnie decided it was time to execute his own plan. First, he would speak to Luigi.

Chapter 37

Tahiti Noveau Hotel and Resort

The red light on the room phone flickered, and it rang softly. Barry looked at it. He had not given anyone his room information. Out of curiosity, he answered.

"Barry, it is me, Fleur. I have some information for you. I spoke to my old school friend. He is the one I mentioned to you, and he is involved with gangs here. He owed me a favor. Can I come up and see you? I can tell you what he has told me."

"Good morning, Fleur. Yes, certainly. Come on up."

Barry admitted Fleur, and they sat together to enjoy coffee and pastries before she advised him of her meeting with a low-level gangster known as 'Bark'.

"He tells me that on the outskirts of town, near the road up to the mountain lookout, there is a gang with an old house. They built a new secure building. The gang is a bunch of cokeheads and drug runners. Not too intelligent. They built that building as a storage area to store items they stole, like TVs, cameras, sound systems, etc. 'Bark' was told by one of them that all the gang members had been prohibited from entering the building. The boss is a convicted murderer named Antoine. He has a wicked reputation. 'Bark' asked about the reason no one is allowed into the building and was told some important people are staying there. He thinks it is your friend, Claude."

"Have you told your father this?"

"No, and 'Bark' will not talk to the police or my father."

"Then how is this information usable?"

"We can go and meet with my father. He will advise us."

Barry quietly considered the options. There were few people he knew in Tahiti, and none who could assist. The last thing he wanted was for that information to be leaked, as he was concerned for Claude's life.

"Fleur, I am going to call Buzz Kutz. He had a long career in law enforcement, and I suspect he will have some advice, then we will go and see your father and Mr Poirer."

Fleur fidgeted with a tissue paper, twisting it and rolling it in her hands. Barry sensed her nervousness.

"What is wrong, Fleur? You seem nervous. Is there more?"

"Yes. 'Bark' is my cousin. He will know I ratted on the gang. I am not sure what he will do, but I will not be safe."

"We will find a way to protect you. They will not know."

His words were interrupted by a loud knocking on the room door. Fleur looked at Barry. Her frightened eyes were the size of saucers. Barry quickly guided her into the bathroom and pulled the door closed.

"Who is there? What do you want? I am resting."

There was silence for several minutes.

"I have information for you. It is about Claude de Passioné.

At hearing Claude's name, Barry rushed to the door and threw it open without hesitation. Standing in the doorway entrance was the man with the strange brown hair and wearing inappropriate heavy clothing. It was Knuckles O'Brien. Barry glared at him.

"Who the hell are you, and what do you want? Are you some two-bit reporter looking for a scoop? I have nothing to say, and I don't know what you are talking about. I am here on business to negotiate a new supply of fish products."

Knuckles let out a long laugh.

"Come on, now, me boy. You are Barry Jones, and a good friend and partner of Claude de Passioné. If you let me in, I will tell you where he is and why he is being held."

Barry ushered him into the room and pointed at the couch.

"Ok. Spill it. What is it you have to tell me, and how much are you looking for?"

"Well, sir. Can't say I will be able to say much without one of them fine whiskeys you have on that bar."

Barry looked at the Irishman in frustration but went to the bar and poured him a large whiskey.

"Now speak."

"Before I do that, I need some protection, and of course, a little money will help."

"If you want to leave here with your head still attached, you will tell me everything. You are in no position to bargain."

Barry pointed the Glock pistol he had brought for his protection at Knuckles.

Knuckles set his glass down and raised his hands.

"No need for that. I simply need to be protected. I will tell you a lot more than where Claude is held. I will explain the reasons for the problems at the winery."

"If what you say is true, then let me bring someone here who will be able to offer you that protection."

He called in the direction of the bathroom.

"Fleur. Come out."

The bathroom door creaked open, and she entered the living area.

"Barry, that is one of the men who were asking around the hotel about you."

"Fleur, I need you to go and bring your father here immediately. Maybe Poirier as well. Hurry."

Fleur ran across the room and left in a hurry.

Approximately 30 minutes later, there was a crash, and the hotel room door flew open. Two soldiers dressed in battle fatigues charged into the room carrying semi-automatic weapons that they pointed at Barry and Knuckles. A full minute passed before Colonel Leclair and Marc Poirier entered.

Colonel Leclair commanded the soldiers to lower their weapons, then frisk Knuckles and guard the door. He glared at Knuckles.

"Mr O'Brien, I am placing you under arrest on the grounds of sabotaging French national interests."

"How do you know my name?"

"We have been watching you since your arrival on the island. Our system flagged you even though you used a false passport. Our facial identity system was not fooled. Once we checked on you, your vast criminal record triggered alarms."

"I came here to speak with Barry Jones. I have important information. I mean no harm to him or Claude de Passioné or his family. I can help you recover Claude and stop the criminal events aimed at crippling the de Passioné family businesses. If Claude does not cooperate with them, they intend to kill him and his mother. You must release me and let me tell you of their plans."

The Colonel conferred with Marc Poirier and then requested one of the soldiers to handcuff Knuckles and seat him at the small room table.

"I will listen. I advise you to tell the truth."

For the next hour, Knuckles told of the plan to collapse the businesses and identified the key figures involved. Colonel Pierre Leclair listened in disbelief.

"If what you say is true, then we need to move quickly. What you say involves threats to both the internal and external interests of France. We, the DGSE and DGSI, will assume control. We will, of course, bring in the local police. Since this involves so many aspects of crime in different countries, we will need to inform Interpol and the FBI. We need to move immediately to rescue Claude. I will contact our tactical Commander, and then you can tell us exactly where he is and describe the place in which they are imprisoned."

The Colonel signaled the soldiers to take Knuckles by the arms and escort him to their headquarters.

Chapter 38

The rescue

Before disclosing all of the details of Claude's location, Knuckles requested and received written confirmation of immunity. The avocats for DGCE initially advised against any release, but after a full briefing, they reluctantly drafted a statement of immunity.

The Commander called in the leaders of the assault force. Knuckles described the location and showed it on a map. He was grilled for details on the building. Finally, the Commander decided they had adequate information to mount an assault.

The Commander turned to the Colonel.

"I recommend we attack under the cover of this evening. That will give my men some time to survey the location in daylight and plan the attack. Our men will be heavily disguised while doing reconnaissance. We don't want to alarm the gang."

"I trust your skills, but we want Claude back unharmed. According to our informant here, he has been drugged."

"Sir, what about the woman he is with?"

"While it is desirable to rescue her, it will be regrettable if she becomes collateral damage. She will have important details of the criminal plans for the de Passionné family. Please use the best efforts of the team to capture her alive."

The afternoon was spent with the Colonel and Marc Poirier interrogating Knuckles, while members of the tactical assault team surveyed the building where Claude was captive. Calls were placed to the liaison for Interpol, and by late afternoon, a team of police, French security forces, and FBI agents attached to the US consulate met for a review of the situation. An agreement was reached on a total blackout of any information to the media until Claude was safe, and the appropriate authorities were briefed. A plan was devised to coordinate, apprehend, and stop the actions of Sir Reginald, Arnie Jacobson, Luigi Fratti, and Lee Chang. The investigation and plans were top secret.

The afternoon slipped by, and at dusk, the assault team gathered. Several nondescript armored vehicles waited for the armed men in the armory. Men wearing battle fatigues, helmets, and night vision goggles climbed into the vehicles.

Colonel Leclair gestured to Barry to join him in the lead vehicle.

"We will stop in a staging area close to the building. Our men will assemble in the dense growth outside the grounds. They will attack very quickly, as there are surveillance cameras located around the perimeter. They will want to create confusion and an element of surprise. The attack and rescue should be over in minutes if successful."

"And if it's not successful?"

"A second group equipped with flash bombs and gas will attack. We want to hit them hard and fast while minimizing the possibility of an all-out gunfight. The second group will shoot to kill without hesitation. They are an elite group trained in hostage rescues."

As they watched from a distance, Barry observed a group of 6 men moving toward the building hidden by the heavy growth of shrubs and bushes. They were carrying a long battering ram. Approximately 20 yards from the door, they grouped and ran at the front door. There was a loud crash as the ram punctured the door. Splinters of wood flew in all directions, and the door flew open.

The men continued into the building amid shouts and gunshots. They targeted the steel door and, using the ram, caved in the steel area around the lock. The door sprang open. Two of the men rushed in and grabbed Claude and Vicky. Seconds later, they emerged half-dragging and half-carrying Claude. Another of the party ran in behind them and pulled Vicky out. The sound of automatic gunfire sounded from the building. Barry watched as another of the team ran forward and lobbed a canister through the smashed doorway. A bright flash illuminated the scene with a loud explosion. Several of the gang ran from the building into the arms of the waiting force. As he watched, Barry noticed a yellow flickering as flames engulfed the front and side of the structure.

The Colonel tapped Barry on the shoulder and pointed to a jeep that had arrived on the scene. He advised Barry that it was time to leave and return to DGCE Headquarters.

By the time they returned to Headquarters, night had fallen. Barry remembered how black the skies were in the Southern Hemisphere as he looked up at the clusters of stars.

Inside the Colonel's office, they discussed the next steps now that Claude had been recovered.

"It is of extreme importance that I get Claude fully briefed on what has happened and the impending actions the criminal syndicate plans. I need to speak with him."

"Barry, I understand the urgency, but we have him in our Military Medical facility here for a complete check. The staff at the facility is all first-class. Most have been in action in some of the most troubled areas in the world. He is in good hands. You must be patient. We should get a report on his condition within an hour or so."

"Pierre, why does France maintain this military presence here in the Pacific? It must be expensive and seems excessive to guard Tahiti."

"Barry, the base is not just for Tahiti. Years ago, we established a major air force operation here. It was followed by an army and then a naval base. France has other islands in the Pacific for whom we are responsible. As an Australian, I am sure you remember the nuclear testing that France performed at an atoll. It caused great political opposition from other countries. Our testing was interrupted by the Greenpeace organization and their radical ways of protest. France was angered, and the Greenpeace ship, 'The Rainbow Warrior', was blown up by our secret service while docked in New Zealand. That sure caused a major political storm."

"Yes, I remember that well. French wines were boycotted, and French restaurants in Sydney and Auckland were closed as protesters targeted them."

"The base here is fully operational and on alert continually. There is concern that in the neighboring islands, there is a lot of political instability. Our job is to be ready in the event any of these regimes threaten any French territory."

The discussion continued and again returned to the topic of returning Claude to France and the business.

"Barry, I am expecting Fleur soon. Would you like to join us for dinner in the officers' mess? I can assure you it is not like the barracks style that is often portrayed in films. It is our private little restaurant."

"It would be my pleasure."

" I am sure she will be here soon. Also, I expect we will have the results of the checkup of Claude before our dinner is over."

Together they sat making small talk until Fleur arrived and then proceeded to the Officer's Mess. It was not as Barry had envisaged it. The mess was a large room partitioned off from the rest of the facility and decorated as a French Bistro. Barry was impressed. Pierre Leclair observed the look of amazement on Barry's face.

"Barry, we have this little perk here for the officers, as many are away from France and home for months on end. It is an attempt to keep morale up. You are going to be surprised when you see the wine list, and yes, we have de Passioné wines."

They selected a table and sat. Fleur led the conversation by suggesting pre-dinner drinks. Barry and Pierre agreed. A very young man dressed in a crisp military uniform approached the table and took the drink order.

As they were enjoying their drinks, a Doctor dressed in a long white coat entered the Mess. The young waiter approached and spoke with him before returning to the table.

"Colonel, Sir. The Doctor requests permission to join you."

The Colonel turned and beckoned the Doctor to approach. The Doctor was in his late 30s. Upon arriving at the table, he saluted the Colonel.

"Relax, Doctor. It is not necessary to be formal. What do you have to report on the patient?"

The Doctor consulted the clipboard he was carrying.

"Considering what he has been through, he is in remarkably good condition. There are some concerns. He has a nasty infection on the side of his neck. We suspect it is from a dirty syringe that was used to inject drugs into him, as there are needle marks evident. To be safe, we gave him a tetanus shot. He is suffering from hypertension and is dehydrated. We are waiting for the full blood test analysis, but the preliminary tests are alarming. His blood shows extreme levels of unknown drugs. We need results from a spectrum analyzer to know what drugs they are. There is, however, one drug that stood out in the tests and is easily identifiable.

The Doctor paused and looked at them all.

"Well, come on, man. Spit it out."

In a low voice, the Doctor spoke.

"He is full of a sexual enhancement drug. It is similar to Viagra except it is in liquid form. We are surprised, given the concentration in his blood, that he doesn't have a permanent erection."

Barry roared out loud, laughing and slapping his hand on his knee, causing others in the room to stare at them as if they were mad.

"Bloody Bonaza, mate. Cor stiffen the bloody crows, you couldn't keep Rajah out of action even in captivity."

The Colonel looked at Barry aghast. The Doctor turned away, and Fleur put her hand to her mouth to suppress her giggles. Barry's fine Australian slang confused them, but it was not wasted on Fleur.

Barry's exuberance was in part due to knowing Claude was fine.

The Colonel composed himself and spoke.

Please see me in my office at 0800 hours tomorrow with a full report on both patients.

Chapter 39

Disturbing news

Sir Reginald was anxious. His calls to Knuckles O'Brien and Vicky were going unanswered. He sensed a problem and wondered whether he should contact the gangsters in Tahiti with whom he had arranged to imprison Claude until they could get him off the island. He did not care about Vicky. She had served her purpose. He decided against alarming the others, but if things continued badly, he would contact Luigi.

The pressure was mounting on him. They were only days from executing the plan, and now this. He called his secretary and demanded that she go out and buy all the latest papers. When she left, he flicked on the TV and scanned the news channels looking for any mention of Claude or strange events happening in Tahiti.

After scanning the news channels, he scoured through the newspapers his secretary had bought. There was no mention of any strange happenings. The few articles on de Passioné were old and contained no new information.

Sir Reginald was frazzled and dreading the call he needed to make to advise the Boss of this latest development. He sat at his desk and went over a checklist of each step they had carefully planned out. He was unable to determine what was wrong.

For a few minutes, he contemplated going to Tahiti himself, but soon discarded that idea. It would set off alarm bells, and the authorities would pay close attention since his name had been in the press articles about the impending failure of the business.

Desperate, Sir Reginald decided to call Luigi.

"Luigi, how are you? I am wondering whether Vicky has contacted you. I am having trouble reaching her since I arranged for Claude and her to be taken somewhere safe and away from others looking for Claude."

"No. When I last spoke to her, everything was good. She was in good spirits, and we discussed taking a vacation together when this is all over."

"I'm trying to reach her on her secure sat phone. Maybe I have a technical issue. Can you try?"

"Hang up. I will try and call you back."

30 minutes passed before Luigi called back.

"I tried, and the number seemed dead. I called the SAT company, and they ran tests for both Vicky's and Knuckles's phones. They advised me that both phones are out of service and possibly damaged."

"This is making no sense."

"What are we going to do? We need contact. Especially now."

"When we first were told of the need to get Claude off the island, I contacted my trustworthy friend and cousin, Antonio (Grease) Bruno. He has already left Hawaii and is on his way to Tahiti. I suspected we may need him, so I acted in advance. Of course, he will want a cut. He has expenses and doesn't work for free."

Silently, Sir Reginald was furious.

" Yet another body added to the group. The more bodies, the harder it will be to control. Someone will talk."

"You can trust me. Bruno will not talk. He has had his adventures."

"I am concerned. Now that Barry Jones is there, he will actively start investigating, and from what I know of him, he is a tenacious person. He won't give up. Expect problems from him."

"I trust Bruno to deal with him. He dealt with problems between warring gangs. He knows how to handle himself."

"I have not discussed this latest development with Arnie, and want to keep it from Lee Chang and the Chinese gang."

"I agree. Until we know more, we should keep things quiet."

The sound of his office door opening startled Sir Reginald. He turned to see Lady Agnes Thwacker entering his office unannounced.

" All right, Luigi. It was kind of you to call. We will speak again soon."

He hung up and looked at Lady Thawcker. She stared at him, and her jet-black eyes, like black diamonds, seemed to look right through him.

"Why were you speaking to Luigi? What did he want? Is there something happening that I don't know about?"

"No, my dear. Luigi has invited us to spend some time at his Villa in Calabria. I think when the deal I am working on closes, we should go."

"I am not going to Italy. They don't even speak English there, too many loud people, strange food, and they eat too much garlic and smell of it."

"Oh, come on. It's not that bad. It will be good for you."

"That's what you said about that godforsaken trip we took to France. No, I am not going to Italy."

"Dear, you seem aggravated. Why don't we go and enjoy some cocktails at the Savoy?"

"As much as I would like that, I have some errands to run. Don't forget we are going to the Princess Alice's in Belgravia tonight. It's her special birthday evening. Don't forget the equipment."

The mention of the party cheered Sir Reginald up immensely. The orgies at Princess Alices were unlike others. She only invited the rich and famous. His mind floated to the memory of the last party there. He recalled the naked bodies all wearing disguises. He looked forward to being able to use his equipment, and he knew who he wanted to share it with.

He walked Lady Thwacker to the door.

" I will see you at home, and we will leave for the party together."

Chapter 40

0800 Hours DGCE HQ Tahiti

Barry had dressed and eaten his breakfast early at the hotel. He was eager to attend Colonel Leclair's office and receive an update on Claude's condition. He had scanned the TV news channels and was pleased there was nothing new relating to the Passioné situation.

He presented himself to the security office at the gates and waited patiently while his arrival and request to visit Colonel Leclair were relayed.

Barry was surprised when the Colonel himself arrived at the gates to admit him. The Colonel went to the desk and signed him into the establishment.

"Good morning, Barry. Let's hope we can get further ahead in dealing with this whole de Passioné matter."

After entering, they walked across a paved yard with various military vehicles and equipment parked.

"I certainly hope so. I will need to contact France and update Buzz and Marie-France. They are worried and deserve to know the latest."

"I agree, but let's wait until we are briefed on Claude and that woman Vicky's condition."

They arrived at the entrance to the office building that housed the Colonel's office. On the way into his office, the Colonel requested coffee be delivered for their meeting with the Doctor.

The Colonel and Barry positioned themselves at opposite ends of two luxurious couches that faced each other and waited. A young junior officer in a crisp uniform arrived with coffee, pastries, and juices.

At exactly 0800, there was a knock on the door, and the Doctor walked in. He turned and extended his hand back through the door and assisted Claude into the room. Barry leaped to his feet and rushed to hug Claude. The Doctor stood and addressed the Colonel.

"Colonel, I think this is the best report I can deliver for you. Claude is in remarkably good condition considering what he has been through. It is going to take at least another 3 days before all those drugs are out of his system. We have the lab report back, and most of the drugs are synthetic sedatives of very poor quality. Provided Claude drinks a significant amount of water and flushes it from his system by taking Furosemide to prevent any fluid buildup, he should be fine. The infection on his neck will heal, and we have prescribed an antibiotic."

"What is the situation with the other patient, Vicky Spanoli?"

"I am afraid the news regarding her is not so positive. She had two bullets that needed removal. Unfortunately, one of the bullets penetrated close to her spine and central nervous system. Likely, she will never walk again. She has lost a lot of blood and is extremely weak. It will be a long recovery for her."

Barry expressed his frustration.

"Damn. We need to interrogate her. She has critical information regarding a major crime that is planned. When can we see her?"

"She is lucid but weak. If you do not question her for too long, I suggest you wait a few hours. She will be medicated with pain relievers but should be able to converse with you."

"Thank you, Doctor. We will arrange to meet in her room two hours from now."

The Doctor nodded and left them. Claude asked Barry to explain all that had happened.

"Not so fast, Claude. I think we need to hear what happened and where you have been. How much do you know?"

"Before we were locked up by that gang, Vicky told me of a plan to take control of the company by an international crime syndicate. I was astounded to learn that investment banker Sir Reginald Coxburn was involved. She did tell me who the others were. If I understand correctly, my family and the estate are in jeopardy. We need to return immediately, as she indicated they were about to proceed within days. I suggest we get our lawyers and bankers together in a meeting. We need to prevent the possibility of them triggering an event that could lead to the investment bankers panicking."

"Claude, can we arrange a meeting by phone? It will take us days to get back to France and get the parties together."

The Colonel interrupted.

"I think that you must understand that the French government will be involved. As it has been explained to me, both the internal and external interests of France are threatened if they force the failure of the companies. The de Passioné name is synonymous with France and French wines. It must be protected. With your permission, Claude, I will initiate the necessary steps for the involvement of our security apparatus. We need to get as much information from Vicky Spagnoli as possible this morning. I agree we must move fast. What services can we offer from here?"

"I need to get access to our secure databases. That can only be done from my office in France. I can contact our IT providers and ask if it is possible to get remote access."

"I will arrange a private office here for you and Barry."

In the privacy of the office, Barry questioned Claude.

"I think you need to explain where you have been and what happened. I will update you on what has happened at the company, but first, I need you to tell me a few things."

"Barry, I wanted to get away from the mess in Rarotonga. There were too many things there for me to deal with. It was hard to learn that I had a young daughter and her existence had been hidden from me for years by Atarangi and her family. Then, there was the kidnapping, and that too was orchestrated by her family. The damages kept growing in our relationship, and then the final blow came in the form of our divorce. I could not focus on business. I decided to return to France after taking a few days in Tahiti to clear my mind. It was during the trip to Tahiti that I met Vicky Spagnoli. We ended up in an intense relationship, which in retrospect was a mistake on my part. I don't know what happened. I experienced strange things. My memory is vague. I remember not feeling well for some time. I wondered if I had experienced some type of breakdown. For unknown reasons, I recently started feeling normal with one exception. I was continually aroused sexually. Later, we were advised to leave the hotel for our safety and taken to a strange location and locked up. I have no recollection of being taken from there to the medical facility here."

“Claude, it will take a while to fully describe all that has happened at the company and the dangerous state of affairs that now exist. I will explain.”

Barry launched into the sabotage at the winery, and then all he had learned from Knucles O’Brian.

Claude had remained silent as Barry relayed all he knew.

“Barry, this is serious. We need to leave here and get back to prevent that syndicate from taking action. I am going to contact our IT people now. There is a 12-hour difference in time, but they are contracted to support us no matter what hour.”

“Claude, we must inform Marie-France and Buzz that you are safe. I also suggest we contact our PR firm immediately and issue a press release indicating you are fine and fell victim to criminal elements while traveling back to France. We need to restore our bankers and supporters' confidence.”

“We have been betrayed by some of those we trusted and who had sensitive information. I need to think about who they may be so we can isolate them from any actions we plan to save the companies.”

They were interrupted by a loud knocking at the office door. Barry opened the door to find Knuckles O’Brienstanding there. He was accompanied by a French MP.

“I wanted to meet Claude and apologize for the actions I took in the past. I had been pressured by Sir Reginald Coxburn. My life was at stake. Claude, I warn you, do not trust him, but it is not just him. He is under the control of another person. I will cooperate with any inquiry or legal action you or your companies take. I am truly sorry.

The MP authoritatively advised Knuckles that the visit was over and he was to be returned to the cell.

Chapter 41

Taking Action

For hours, Claude and Barry reviewed the plans they had made. Lists of people critical for preventing the collapse were prepared. Claude had contacted the IT company in France but was awaiting a call from their senior management, as his requests exceeded the authority of the staff he had spoken with.

Barry contacted their public relations company to issue an immediate release and then contacted the local media in Tahiti.

Upon hearing that Claude was safe, Buzz sprang into action in France and contacted the major TV network news operations. Marie-France was elated and announced she would be acquiring a new wardrobe to welcome Claude home.

Claude hoped the flurry and intensity of the news surrounding his capture and release would panic the syndicate and stop any actions they had in progress.

Tired, Claude and Barry decided to take a break and leave the office for lunch at a local restaurant. On their way out, Barry decided to stop at the Colonel's office and invite him. The adjutant outside the Colonel's inner office left to announce Barry and Claude's presence. He returned and showed them into the office. Barry was surprised to see Fleur standing and talking to her father. The Colonel stood and introduced Claude to Fleur. She shook Claude's hand, and it was obvious that whatever attraction she had previously had for Barry was replaced by the tanned athletic man in front of her. There was no delay in her accepting the invitation to lunch. She prodded her father to join them.

"Come on, father. It's my last afternoon here before I leave to return to the States."

Barry frowned on hearing of her planned departure.

"Yes, I will fly back early this evening as I will have exams soon at the university."

At the restaurant, the talk was mainly about life in France, university in California, and the wine business. Claude and Barry stayed off the subject that they all knew was on everyone's mind.

Barry observed the flirtatious looks Fleur made at Claude. He couldn't help but smile if she only knew of his overdosed erotic condition. Even under adverse situations, Claude attracted the women. He wondered if Claude realized it.

They finished lunch and headed back to the office. Claude was eager to complete matters with the IT company and prepare to meet with his key people.

Back at the office, they said farewell to Fleur. She gave Barry a smile and handshake but hugged Claude and invited him to contact her when he was next in California. Barry realized the move had been made.

When they were alone in the private office, Barry spoke to Claude.

"Claude. There is one thing I have not mentioned. The syndicate planned to kidnap Marie-France and hold her ransom until you signed over the ownership of the estate and business. If that were to fail for any reason, the backup plan is for you to be killed, after which steps will automatically be taken to pass the ownership to the investors. You are not safe. We need to be very careful.

In Italy, the news of Claude's escape infuriated Luigi Fratti. He thought of all the financial moves he had schemed up with Vicky and Arnie Jacobson. Vicky was the key player and had brought Sir Reginald and Arnie together. Through a series of transactions with both financial institutions, he had been able to successfully launder millions of dollars from his drug trafficking business. It had been during Vicky's trip to Calabria that she had proposed the plan to take over de Passioné wineries and family holdings. Her plan seemed foolproof. All the components were there. The financial vehicles were in place, and their principals were more than willing to participate.

Now it was a mess. Luigi was frustrated. He had noticed an increased control of the syndicate over the past few months by Sir Reginald. It confused him. Sir Reginald made suggestions and agreed with the others, but he never acted himself. It seemed he was deferring the decisions to another.

The trust Luigi had in Sir Reginald was all but non-existent. He refrained from contacting him, instead considering what actions the others would want to take, given the recent developments.

Luigi decided against taking any action or contact and would wait until the other members contacted him. In his mind, he had an idea that would solve the problem. He was not prepared to share it without some form of remuneration. He resolved to wait…no matter how long.

Back at the DGCE office in Tahiti, Claude and Barry continued contacting the parties they believed could prevent the syndicate from achieving their goal.

It was mid-afternoon when Claude received a return call from the IT company in France. He described his need to obtain remote access to the highly secured servers containing both corporate and family accounts. He listened as it was explained that it was not possible. After some discussion, a solution was found. It was possible to establish a secure VPN (Virtual Private Network) link to the de Passioné servers in the de Passioné California offices. Claude immediately agreed. There was one complication. The physical VPN security device was in France. Claude did not want to risk it with a courier service. He called Buzz in France.

"Buzz, I need you to meet Barry and me in San Francisco as soon as possible. I need you to bring the network security key from the safe in my office. The timing is critical. I am making arrangements to fly there as soon as possible. I will contact you with our flight information when I have it.

"Barry, we are going to California. I will ask the Colonel for his assistance to get us on a flight."

After hearing of Claude's need to get to California without delay, the Colonel requested his adjutant to check all flights, military and commercial, headed to San Francisco and Oakland.

"Sir, your daughter is on a government flight early this evening. I can secure seats for your guests."

"Do it, please. Remember they are VIP and should be treated as such., Please make the arrangements and advise Claude and Barry."

An hour later, the door to the private office opened, and Denis Ricard joined them.

"I understand you will be leaving soon. I had hoped we would have had more time together, but I understand the importance of your return. I will see you in France soon. I am planning a visit and vacation with my wife, Guylaine. We will take the wine tours via the barges that sail the canals and stop at different wineries and restaurants. We are looking forward to the trip. Until then, I wish you both well."

The Colonel arranged a car to take them to the airfield for the flight. On the way, Barry stopped at the hotel for his clothing and business papers.

It was night when the flight soared into the air. After the flight leveled off, Claude excused himself and went to sit with Fleur. Barry shook his head. It seemed Claude would never learn.

Chapter 42

California.

The plane descended into San Francisco as the dawn was breaking. Barry immediately arranged a room at the Hyatt in downtown San Francisco where they could rest, work, and wait for the arrival of Buzz, who was expected early afternoon after the 12-hour flight from Paris.

Claude asked for Fleur's contact information before they separated at the airport. Fleur was eager to give it to him.

In their room, Claude made numerous phone calls, assuring people he was fine and returning to the company. Many were relieved to hear of his return.

One of the calls he made was to the director responsible for the de Passioné winery in Napa Valley. He advised the director of his plans to arrive there that evening and for him to arrange accommodation for Buzz, Barry, and himself. He also requested that the IT personnel be available to assist in linking the California operation with France.

He and Barry left for an early lunch over which they compiled a list of the most critical people to invite to a meeting on saving the de Passioné businesses. With the list complete, Claude contacted Horatio Henderson.

"Horatio, it is good to be able to speak with you again. I understand that during a forensic audit of the businesses, your people have uncovered some anomalies. I am convening a meeting of the most important stakeholders at our offices here in California. I would like you to fly out and meet me as soon as you can. After this evening, I will be contactable through the offices here."

"There are indeed some very serious issues we have found. A number are illegal and violate several Securities Commission regulations. To complicate matters, these violations involve jurisdictions outside the US. Without disclosure and remedial actions, you are liable. We need to get not only our bankers placated, but we need the authorities to be on our side as well. The legal authorities in those other regions will need to cooperate with the US Securities Commission. Many offshore transactions include illegal transfers, money laundering, transfers to restricted parties, and more. It is a mess, but was cleverly hidden. I suggest you make it a priority to get your lawyers active. Make sure they attend your meetings. I will leave and be there tomorrow afternoon."

With lunch concluded and the lists prepared, Claude decided he needed to take a walk around Fisherman's Wharf and clear his head after all that had happened.

People milled around to watch the street performers with their magic tricks and music. He stood and listened to the musicians busking. He laughed at some of the conjuring tricks performed with sleight of hand. The longer he stayed watching, the less the stress weighed on him. Barry was pleased to see Claude relaxing a little.

Upon returning to the hotel, they found Buzz waiting for them. After a hurried meeting, it was decided to travel that evening to the de Passioné estate in Napa.

Barry requested the concierge to assist in arranging an executive rental car for them to drive to Napa Valley. Within the hour, Exec-u-Rental delivered a new Lincoln Continental for their use.

Buzz showered and freshened up after the flight from France. After a light meal, they packed, checked out of the hotel, and proceeded to leave for Napa.

Chapter 43

Ambush, Pacific Coast Highway, California

The afternoon light was fading, and the sky was a radiant orange as the setting sun's rays reflected off the clouds and dropped below the horizon of the Pacific Ocean.

Lissa J. loved this time of the day and the drive north to Napa Valley. She had arranged a weekend away in Napa, touring the various wineries with her friends, and was anxious to reach the Inn at Russian River.

While driving over the Golden Gate Bridge from San Francisco in her favorite Jeep, Lissa had the radio turned loud and sang along with Duran Duran's 'Planet Earth.' Tired of the song and facing the long drive, she settled back and hummed a tune she had learned and sung as a toddler. Whenever she was alone and stressed, she would sing or hum the song, Tanya Tucker's Delta Dawn.

The traffic was light, and she stayed behind a dark-colored Lincoln. Having previously been ticketed for speeding and cognizant of the high fines in California, Lissa stuck to the speed limit and was thankful the Lincoln in front of her was also adhering to the limit. It made the drive less stressful.

She followed the Lincoln as it proceeded up the coast road. The first signs of dusk were setting in. Darkness would soon envelop the rural area of the coast road she was driving through.

The chill of the early spring air cooled the Jeep, and Lissa reached over and killed the air conditioning. She continued to hum and only paused when the bright LED headlights from a following vehicle reflected in her mirror and blinded her. She raised her hand to shield the mirror and noticed the vehicle was traveling at a high speed and was intent on passing her. She pulled to the right to allow the vehicle by. A large shiny black Chevy SUV blasted past her. She watched as it gained distance on the Lincoln. Lissa was concerned and immediately dropped back a little. She watched in horror as the SUV swung into the oncoming traffic lane and drew parallel with the Lincoln. Brake lights flashed on the SUV, and it turned into the rear side of the Lincoln, forcing it off the road. The Lincoln mounted the grassy shoulder and flipped over several times. Lissa hit the brakes of the Jeep and screeched to a halt as the SUV accelerated away from the scene. She unbuckled and jumped from the Jeep and ran toward the overturned Lincoln.

Steam hissed out from the front of the car, and a dirty grey smoke curled from the trunk. Lissa bent and looked in through the broken glass of the driver's window. She observed two occupants. The driver hung from his seat, partially suspended by his seatbelt. Blood covered his face and gushed from his neck. Lissa pulled open the door enough to allow her to release the seatbelt. She pulled the inert body from the car and dragged it a distance from the wreck before returning to extricate the passenger. He was larger and heavier but had been thrown forward as the car rolled, making it easier for her to pull him from the wreck. He, too, was drenched with blood. Lissa tried to move him away from the wreck but noticed his arm fell limply by his side, and she was unable to get a grip and pull him using that arm. As she gained distance from the wreck, there was a roar as flames leaped into the air.

Several cars had stopped, and people ran to assist her. An 18-wheel transport truck rolled to a stop, and the driver jumped from the cab carrying a fire extinguisher. He raced to the wreck and drenched it with a fire suppressant foam. The flames receded, and an acrid smoke drifted from the wrecked car. The driver assisted in pulling the passenger from the wreckage.

Someone had dialed 911, and the sound of wailing sirens from the approaching police cars and ambulance could be heard in the distance.

Several people were assisting the truck driver to apply a tourniquet to the driver's leg. A massive amount of blood had seeped from him and saturated the ground around his body. Others were trying to assist the unconscious passenger.

A California Highway Patrol pulled to a stop next to Lissa's Jeep. A sergeant and a young officer exited the car and walked down to the scene of the wreck.

"Any witnesses to what happened here?" the sergeant asked.

Lissa replied, and the sergeant listened as she recalled the incident. While she was describing the accident, the young cop took out his high-power flashlight and shone it over the wreck. He noted down the license plate numbers and returned to the patrol car and radioed them in. Minutes passed until the radio crackled a response. The young officer listened and then excitedly ran to the sergeant,

"Sir, you need to hear this. That car is a rental and rented to the de Passioné company."

The sergeant quickly approached the injured driver and shone his flashlight on the man's face.

"My God. I think it is Claude de Passioné. We need to get him into the ambulance and to the hospital without delay."

Upon arrival, the EMTs ran down to Claude and started to assess the situation. Seeing the other injured man, an EMT radioed for another ambulance to attend the scene urgently.

While the EMTs were attempting to place Claude on a stretcher, he incoherently mumbled. The sergeant and EMTs tried to understand the garbled words.

"Ari, ari, ari"

When the attendants went to lift the stretcher, Claude feebly attempted to raise his head and continued mumbling "ari, ari, ari"

One of the EMTs took a syringe and injected a sedative to relieve his shock and pain. Within seconds, Claude passed out and was whisked away to the area hospital.

The second ambulance arrived, and after assessing his situation, the passenger was also taken to the hospital, but his identity was unknown.

The sergeant cursed as he took in the scene of the burned car and the assembled crowd who had gathered.

"Just what we don't need here in our sleepy little town. An accident involving a de Passioné will bring in hordes of media hounds because of that family's recent troubles and scandals. I need to get this incident reported immediately before the press picks up on it."

The young cop looked troubled.

"What do you think he was trying to tell us? Who or what is 'ari', and why was the rear passenger side door wrenched open? There are burnt and damaged business documents and a briefcase on the floor. It seems strange that there was nothing like that in front of the car. I am going to check around."

Another police car from the State Police pulled up and proceeded to receive a debrief from the sergeant. At the mention of Claude de

Passioné, the senior officer left to contact his superiors. He returned a few minutes later and advised the sergeant that no one was to touch anything as the accident had been labeled a crime scene and that the local police would be posting officers until a forensic team arrived and documented the scene."

A shout rang out as the young cop called for assistance. The sergeant and the State troopers ran toward the area where the young cop stood shouting and pointing up at a tree. One of the State troopers shone his high-power flashlight at the tree. The body of Barry Jones was draped between the branches.

As the group of cops stood discussing ways to retrieve the body, two men in dark suits approached, with one flashing a badge.

"We are with the FBI. We will be assuming control as the victims in this accident are involved in an active, high-profile investigation. We will want to interview any witnesses and request access to your reports. We cannot disclose the nature of our investigation, but we can assure you it is active at the highest level in our country and involves the CIA and law enforcement internationally. All attending officers are bound to maintain secrecy regarding what has happened here and what has been found. We wish to work with you all and the local authorities to investigate this matter. Who is the witness? What was seen? Where is the witness now?"

The young cop looked at the sergeant before replying.

"Sir, her name is Lissa J. She is in a state of shock and sitting in my cruiser. The ambulance EMTs checked her and gave her a mild sedative. She refused any further medical attention or to be taken to the hospital."

" Accompany me to her. I wish to meet her. We are used to dealing with people in situations like this. We will be gentle with her. I suggest that you return after introducing me and assist in determining the identities of those other passengers."

The young cop walked beside the FBI agent to his cruiser. He was shocked to find the car empty and Lissa J. gone."

Chapter 44

The Witness.

The young cop swore. Lissa was not in the car. He realized he should have seated her in the rear of the car, where the doors could not be opened from the inside. He was expecting a tirade from the FBI agent, but was surprised to hear laughter. He looked around to see Lissa J. walking back toward them with a smile on her face.

"Sorry, officer. I needed to pee and didn't want to make a mess in your car."

The FBI agent turned to the young cop.

" Make that a lesson for you about securing witnesses and suspects. Luckily, I knew she was here as I spotted her silhouette squatting over by that tree. Now don't go and try to do that California thing and cite her for urinating in a public place. We are going to need her help."

Within minutes, the three of them were laughing at the absurdity of the situation, but the laughter subsided when the focus returned to the accident and the victims.

"Thank you, officer. I will take over here and spend some time with the witness. Lissa, is there anything we can get you?"

"No, thank you. I just want to go and meet my friends. They are expecting me and will be worried."

"Don't worry about that. Give me the information where you are staying or meeting them, and I will have local law enforcement contact them and explain that you are with us as an important witness to an accident. Hopefully, we will be able to conclude our questioning quickly, and you will be on your way. We will arrange an escort if required."

"Will I be able to leave soon?"

"We will take a preliminary witness statement, but you will be required to attend for a full, detailed account of the accident. You will be advised of the day and time. If you require assistance to be at that questioning, we will assist you. I request that you do not discuss the details of what you witnessed with anyone. What you have seen was a crime committed by a powerful underworld syndicate. Stay quiet for your safety. More will be explained to you later."

Lissa looked at him before speaking.

"I do not know your name or position."

"I am Special Agent Con Fox, FBI Major Crimes Section (Federal) based in Oakland, California. I am assigned to a case involving the wealthy de Passioné family. Their businesses here in California fall into our jurisdiction."

"What do you want from me?"

" I can not disclose much at this time, but what you witnessed was an attempt to assassinate a person who is the target of an international crime syndicate. We have been investigating this group for months now. Due to their activities outside the US, the CIA is involved, along with law enforcement, in several countries. Your witness statement will be valuable as we have not been able to find any direct evidence of actions they have taken against the target."

Lissa sat quietly thinking before speaking.

"Am I in any danger if I speak with you and provide a witness statement?"

"No. You will receive protection."

Lissa sat quietly for several more minutes.

" If I just gave you the video from my dashcam, would that be enough, then I wouldn't need to give you that statement?"

Agent Fox couldn't believe his luck.

"You have a video recording of the attempted assassination? That will be invaluable. Can we take the video now? It must be kept safe. You are going to be of big help to us. Wait here while I confer with my partner."

Without hesitation, Agent Fox turned and left in the direction of the gathered cops. Upon reaching them, she watched as he pulled aside another tall man. They stood in deep conversation, looking across in her direction every few minutes. Finally, the tall man nodded his head, and then Agent Fox headed back toward her.

"Can you give me the video, please? My partner is senior to me and has agreed that you are free to leave. I will need all your contact information."

Lissa and Agent Fox exchanged information and the video. With the transaction complete, Lissa continued on her way, pleased to be leaving the scene of the wreckage and crowd of rubberneckers.

Darkness had fallen. She drove on and soon reached a small town and slowed her speed down, knowing that often the police were in wait to catch unsuspecting drivers unaware of the speed reductions that often existed. At that hour, the town was asleep. Except for a burger joint and a gas station, everything else was closed. As she exited the town, she accelerated. Traffic was light. Shortly after leaving the town, she noticed a pair of bright LED lights on a vehicle driving a distance behind her. Slowly, the distance between her and the following vehicle closed. She slowed as the brightness of the lights was disturbing her. Suddenly, the vehicle pulled out behind her to pass. A black shiny Chevy SUV pulled alongside her. She glanced at the SUV, but in the darkness, and with its dark-tinted windows, she was unable to see the occupants. The SUV slowed to the same speed and remained alongside her. Fear crept into her mind as she was certain these were the same individuals who had forced the Lincoln off the road.

The SUV remained alongside for what seemed like ages, then, without warning, accelerated away at high speed. Lissa found herself sweating with fear. She was certain it was them and wondered if they were waiting ahead to intercept her. Panic set in. She was driving alone on a rural country road with very few houses. The road was dark. She slowed and looked for a place to stop and request assistance. After several miles, she saw an old farmhouse set a long way back from the road and turned into the gravel driveway. A light was shining in the front window. As she stopped beside the front porch, the outside light turned on and the front door sprang open. A burly man dressed in coveralls and carrying a rifle stood in the doorway.

"Who are you, and what do you want on my property?"

Lissa lowered her window and called back to the man.

"I need help. I am possibly in danger. Some men in a car were acting in a threatening manner. I came in here to hide from them and ask for help. Will you call the police for me?"

The man on the porch lowered his rifle.

"Well, I guess you came to the right place. My son is the county sheriff. I can call him now. Get out of your Jeep slowly and walk up the stairs. I need to be sure you are not armed or plotting some nasty surprise. Are you all alone?"

Lissa slowly climbed out of the Jeep, keeping her hands visible, and walked toward the faded old wooden stairs.

"Yes, sir. I am alone."

He beckoned her to climb the stairs, and as she was doing so, a loud crash sounded from within the house. The man shook his head and laughed.

"Godamn it. That wife of mine is determined to smash all our plates."

Lissa reached the top of the stairs and walked along the porch to where he stood.

"Lucille, we have a visitor. Come on out." He shouted, and seconds later, a round-faced smiling woman appeared. Lissa felt great relief and burst into tears. The events of the night had caught up to her.

"Don't cry, dear. Come in and tell me what the problem is."

As Lucille guided Lissa to the kitchen, she heard the man calling his son and asking him to come to the house, while Lucille asked for details of the problem. Lissa felt trapped as she remembered Agent Fox's instruction not to discuss the details.

"Can we wait till your son arrives, and I will explain, since he is in law enforcement?

"Yes, of course. I will make us a fresh coffee while we wait. He is only a few minutes away."

Lissa sat with Lucille and her husband in the front room of the house, making small talk, sipping coffee, and waiting for the son to arrive. They didn't need to wait long before the lights of a police car turned into the driveway and sped up to the house.

A lanky man unwound himself from the driver's seat and proceeded up the stairs. Within seconds, the door flew open, and he walked in.

"Evening. What's going on? What is the problem?"

The sheriff suddenly stopped speaking and stared at Lissa.

"I've seen you before, Missy. Weren't you at that accident scene a few miles back? Saw you talking to the Feebies."

"Yes, that was me. They have requested I not discuss the accident and what I saw."

"So why are you here with my parents?"

Tears welled up in her eyes as she described the incident with the black SUV and her belief that it was the same vehicle that caused the accident.

"Damn it. No dearie. I believe that's them Cooper brothers out there terrorizing people again in that new black Chevy SUV. Sooner them boys get locked up again, the better. Before they get somebody killed with those chicken games on the road. Guess I need to go and pay them a visit. Don't worry, Missy. There just local yahoos."

Lissa relaxed, but she wondered if the criminal syndicate had hired some locals to do the dirty work.

"Where are you heading tonight, Missy?"

"I am driving to the Russian River to meet my friends."

"That's still a long way to travel alone. My deputy lives up near there. He is about to end his day. I will ask him to travel behind you as an escort."

Lissa was overcome by the friendliness of the strangers.

" I appreciate that."

"OK. Follow me back to my office and meet Vernon. He will be the one accompanying you."

Lissa nodded, but at the same time wondered whether there was anything to be wary of. It all seemed too good to her."

She followed the cop for several miles before turning into a dimly lit, low building.

The cop parked beneath an overhead light and beckoned for her to join him. Together, they entered the station. A thin rail of a man was sleeping at a desk. The cop banged his foot down on the floor, startling the other cop awake.

"Vernon, I need you to accompany this young lady up to the Russian River. Seems those Cooper Brothers were tormenting her earlier. Think I'll go pay them boys a visit."

"Well, that's a problem. That wife of mine got us some tickets to that Country Western concert over there in Bodega Bay. I agreed to pick up her cousins to join us, so I won't be driving north tonight. Sorry, Chief. I'm already late. I had expected to be off shift an hour ago."

The cop turned to Lissa.

"Sorry, but nothing I can do about that. You are on your own. Be careful. It's a safe area, so you should be fine."

Chapter 45

Calabria, Italy

Luigi Fratti was furious. All morning, he had seen news reports of the rescue of Claude de Passioné and an unknown woman. He had tried contacting Sir Reginald Coxburn, but his calls went unanswered. He finally decided to contact Arnie Jacobson.

"Arnie, what happened? When I spoke to Reginald, he assured me that they had been moved to a location controlled by a gang. The location was out of the way and secure. How did this happen? I cannot reach Reginald. Has he been in contact with you?"

"No. I have also attempted to contact him. I have gone as far as sending messages through one of the traders we both work with. Someone secure and private. He responded that he had not seen Reginald for a day."

"Things are bad. The French security in Tahiti is involved. If we are to succeed, we will need to move quickly. There is now a level of risk that, if I had known, I would never have become involved. They will be piecing together Claude's actions since he arrived in Tahiti. They will discover where he stayed and will find out about Vicky Spagnoli. I am worried they will enlist US authorities to examine the recent finances of Sir Reginald and your firm as they relate to Claude and his business. I can contact my sources in the Italian system and try to find out what, if anything, is happening here. My people here are very loyal to me. They cannot afford to be otherwise."

"I would not panic. The funds you and I 'managed' are well disguised. All the appropriate documentation was filed. On the surface, everything is legal."

Luigi was not convinced.

"Arnie, I am uncomfortable. You have control over millions of my dollars. I need your assurance that it will be shielded from any problems that may arise due to this scheme of Sir Reginald."

"Luigi, I must remind you that it was you who originally sent Vicky to Sir Reginald. You and she had devised the de Passioné project. You knew the risks. And selected him as a partner. I remind you that you have also created another concern for us. You brought in those Chinese mobsters. Lee Chang is part of the Tong gang, and you know who some of the other members are, including the notorious and bloodthirsty Ming Hoe. That is something I would never have done. They cannot be trusted."

"I don't need a lecture from you on how to do business. I suggest you find Sir Nigel and find out where Claude de Passioné is."

Luigi hung up in a temper. He needed a distraction to calm him. He wished that Bianca Barbieri were still his mistress. As he thought about her death, his temper grew. Such a waste.

As he turned to leave his office, he was alerted to a newsflash about to be broadcast on RAI, the Italian government-owned TV network. Out of curiosity, he stopped and watched. Shock and surprise hit him when the cameras focused on Claude de Passioné sitting in a comfortable studio chair with a reporter about to interview him. He looked at the caption. The interview was a day old and filmed in San Francisco. Nonetheless, he sat to listen.

Claude deliberately steered the interviewer away from the question of his disappearance. He told the interviewer he had distanced himself in isolation for personal reasons. He continued that it was time for him to return to the family business as they had plans for expansion and a new winery. There was no mention of his abduction. The harder the interviewer pressed, the more casual Claude's response was. Claude assured the viewers that everything was in good order with the business and dismissed the current rumors as a plan concocted by his competition to harm the family. Frustrated, the interviewer thanked him and ended the report.

Luigi considered it a masterful performance to deflect the reality.

As he was about to leave his office, his satellite phone rang. He answered a distressed and incoherent Sir Reginald Coxburn.

"Reggie, calm down. What has happened?"

"Bad news. Lee Chang has caused us a serious problem. He found out that Claude was in San Francisco with Barry Jones and Buzz Kutz. His members in the Tong gang have members working at the Hyatt. Claude did not attempt to disguise his arrival there. The gang was able to learn that Barry Jones had rented a car to drive up to the de Passioné vineyards in Napa Valley. Luigi had told him there was a failsafe provision if Claude refused to cooperate, and that was to kill Claude. Without consulting us, Lee Chang gave orders for his men to follow and kill Claude, Barry, and Buzz. The men caused an accident. They forced the car off the road. From reports, it was a bad accident. There has been no report of fatalities. Photos of the accident scene show a badly smashed car. There are cops everywhere. Local police, State Police, and some plainclothes officers who look to be FBI or others. This is a disaster."

"I knew it. Those fucking Chinese. What do we do now? This wasn't in the plan."

" I need to find out if they are alive. I will try to find out to which hospital they were taken."

Luigi considered the issue.

"You had better hope they are dead, then we can trigger the provisions to start our processes for collapsing the company's finances and support."

"And if they survived, what do we do then?"

" I suggest we involve Arnie to decide that. Have you contacted him? Does he know about this?"

"No. I called you first. Where is Vicky Spagnoli? There has been no mention of the woman Claude was seen with. The other troubling matter is Knuckles O'Brian. He is missing as well."

"Arnie is not going to be pleased. I suggest you find your contacts in California, and if they are not dead, I suggest you arrange it, or you may find yourself and Tantamore Capital joining them."

Luigi's mood continued to darken.

"Luigi, I did my best. I arranged for them to move to a safe location. I don't know how they were found. Someone betrayed us."

"Reggie, old boy. I don't give a fuck. I will destroy you if this fails and I suffer any consequences. I cannot be any clearer. I will take every penny you own and destroy you."

At his office in London, Sir Reginald paled as he was fully aware of the influence Luigi possessed over the gangs in Italy and abroad.

"I will contact Arnie. I suggest we confer soon and decide on a plan."

" Don't call me for a while. I am tired and annoyed. I am going to my favorite restaurant here and enjoying a meal of saltimbocca and some fine wines. Maybe then I will be in a better mood and able to suggest some solutions for this mess."

Sir Reginald hung up. He went to the private bar in his office, poured himself a large Scotch, and returned to sit on the couch looking out at the Thames through the high glass windows. Moments after he settled into the couch, the door opened and Lady Agnes Thwacker walked in.

"Reggie, I saw the news on TV. Our favorite client is back."

She raised her glass in a mock toast.

Chapter 46

Sonoma Valley Hospital

The two ambulances turned into the Emergency Department entrance, sirens wailing. They were followed by a sheriff's car. Attendants hurried out to remove the gurneys on which lay the bodies of Claude and Buzz Kutz.

A triage nurse assessed their state before assigning them to different cubicles.

Buzz was unconscious, whereas Claude was in a dazed state and murmuring incoherently. Each was examined by the young resident doctors. Nurses were called to clean the blood and grime from the men.

The sheriff opened the rear door and assisted a groggy Barry Jones from the car. Barry pushed back in an attempt to refuse assistance. The Emergency nurses were not amused.

"Sir, please let us help. You have been in a bad accident. There may be invisible injuries. We need to examine you."

"Where are the others? What have you done with them? Are they dead?"

"Your friends are receiving treatments already. They are alive, but both suffered injuries."

"Can I see them?"

"No. Not yet. One is in a dazed state and incoherent. The other has some broken bones. They may be admitted."

"I need to see them, especially Claude."

"He is the one who is in a coma. I suggest you be patient. There is nothing we can do at this time other than wait. In the meantime, let's get you examined."

Begrudgingly, Barry agreed. He was stripped of his clothing and placed on a hospital bed.

"What on earth happened with you? The others have injuries associated with car accidents, but you have a couple of strange issues."

"I'm not surprised. I was thrown out of the car and ended up at the top of a tree. So what's the issue? Have I got a branch up my arse?"

The attending doctor and nurse were unable to suppress their laughter.

"Not exactly, but you do have some splintered wood in various locations and close to the area you just mentioned. To prevent infection, we are going to need to remove those pieces."

"Not bloody likely, mate."

"You don't have much of an option. We can remove them while you are sedated to deal with a more serious issue. The cause of your frontal bleeding. Your scrotum is torn, and we will need to stitch it back together."

Barry paled and stared at the doctor in horror.

"You mean you're going put a needle in my dick?"

"I will check and see if we will sew it or use staples."

That was the last straw for Barry. He leaped from the bed and, with the hospital gown flowing behind him, escaped the ward's corridor, only to be stopped by a huge security guard and escorted back to the room.

Barry's rough-and-tumble Australian bravado faded.

"Doctor, will this hurt? Will I be able to leave soon? I need to attend to a critical matter. I can return later or tomorrow."

"No, we will sedate you. You will recover in a few hours. You cannot leave with an open wound like that. Your other injuries are not so serious. Severe bruising in the rib area. We will take some X-rays as well.

Resigned to his fate, Barry gave up his protest.

"Can I please see Claude before the procedure?"

"I will check for you."

As the doctor left, a young nurse entered carrying a tray, which she set down on the bed and then drew the privacy curtain across to enclose the cubicle.

"Now, Barry, this is pretty simple. I need to shave you before the procedure, so lift that gown, please."

Barry's eyes widened. His day was not ending the way he had expected.

After 15 minutes, the doctor returned.

"Barry, who can we contact regarding your friend Barry? He has been trying to say something since he arrived. The EMTs who were at the accident scene say he was doing it there."

"What is he saying?"

"It's something like 'ari ari'. We do not understand."

"I am his closest friend and contact. His mother would be incapable of handling this news. As soon as you can, take me to see him."

"We will go now. Before your procedure. Walking will be a bit difficult for you after."

The doctor led Barry away and through several hospital corridors to a private room where Claude lay hooked up to monitors and a mass of tubes.

As they entered, Claude turned his head toward them. On seeing Barry, he attempted to sit. A nurse reached him and prevented him from sitting up. Claude pointed at Barry and again tried calling out.

Barry moved close to the bed and lowered his head to listen. The words tumbled out.

"ari ari"

Barry stood back and smiled.

"I understand him. He was calling my name Barry Barry."

A different doctor approached them and spoke to both Barry and the doctor accompanying him.

"I need him to rest. We are waiting for some test results, and an MRI is scheduled. He will be staying here for the night."

Before they could leave, Claude became agitated and attempted to speak to Barry, who again leaned down to hear him.

"The device. The device."

Suddenly, Barry understood. The security device he had carried from France would allow secure access between the California and French office systems. Barry realized it was still in the car at the crash site.

"Doctor, is that sheriff still here?"

"I believe he is at reception handling some paperwork."

"I must see him. He cannot leave."

Together, they slowly walked to the reception area, as Barry's condition was worsening.

"Sheriff, there is an urgent matter I need you to assist with."

Barry provided a detailed account of the need for the case containing the security device and asked him to contact the FBI agents who were at the scene.

After a short wait, the FBI agents confirmed they had retrieved the case and would transport it to the hospital.

Barry sighed with huge relief and then surrendered his body and prized privates to the doctor.

Chapter 47

An Unwelcome Confrontation.

Lissa was tired. Her adrenaline rush had faded since leaving the accident scene and the farmer's house. She had been disappointed that the deputy sheriff was not able to escort her on the drive. She had driven toward the Russian River without noticing many of the places she passed. She was yawning and had a sleepy feeling hitting her. Her eyes flickered shut. Forcing them open, she decided to stop at the next coffee shop.

The road dipped down into a small valley. A single-story building with a garish, bright flashing sign advertised the 'World's Best Coffee and Bagels'. Lissa saw gas pumps and decided to stop, refuel, and rest for a while. She pulled alongside a pump, slid in her credit card, and filled her Jeep. When done, she parked and went inside to order a coffee.

The night air was cool, and there was slight condensation on the windows. Lissa sat thinking. Her mind was miles away, recalling her most recent vacation in the Caribbean. She didn't notice the arrival of the black SUV, nor the occupants walking around her car and recording her license plate. The two men, dressed all in black with hoodies pulled back, entered the little coffee shop and examined the occupants. The taller of the two nudged his partner and nodded his head toward Lissa. She did not see his gesture.

The two men sat at a table where they had a clear view of Lissa and spoke. Lissa looked up at them and smiled. She did not understand the language they spoke, but watched and listened, realizing it was Chinese. She shrugged and returned to studying the little map to find the hotel where her friends were waiting.

After finishing her coffee and paying the cashier, she returned to her Jeep but was surprised to see it blocked by the black SUV. She noticed the large dented area where the SUV had pushed the Lincoln off the road. She abandoned her plan to re-enter the shop and to ask the owners to move. They had recognized her car as the one that had witnessed the incident. Lissa calmly walked away into a dense growth of shrubs, took the card for FBI agent Con Fox from her wallet, and called him. After a quick explanation, the FBI agent advised her to stay hidden and that he would have other agents come to her assistance.

Minutes passed. She remained huddled in the growth, the cold penetrating the thin clothing she had chosen for her vacation. A nondescript Ford turned into the parking lot and stopped. Two young men, dressed in fishing gear, exited the car and looked around before one walked to the door of the coffee shop. The other waited by the car. Lissa's phone buzzed.

"Lissa, it's Con. Let the agent know where you are. You are safe."

Lissa emerged from the bushes. As she did, there was a crash as the door of the shop flew open and the agent exited, scuffling with one of the Chinese men.

The second man emerged with a gun in his hand, shouting. Gunshots rang out. The scuffling agent fell to the ground. Both men ran for the SUV. The other agent fired at the SUV, managing to disable it. He ran to the SUV with an automatic assault rifle pointed at the cabin. One of the Chinese fired. Moments later, bullets from the agent's rifle riddled the door. Smoke drifted from inside the SUV. Slowly, the door opened, and the shorter, plump man exited. He raised his hands. The agent ran to him and roughly handcuffed him to the vehicle's bumper. He then ran to assist his partner, who was writhing in pain on the ground. He radioed for help and then ran back to the SUV, where he found the taller of the two Chinese dead on the front seat.

As the agents were taking the handcuffed man to their car, they passed close by Lissa. The man turned to Lissa and spat.

"You better be careful. We know you. We know where you live. We'll kill you if you say anything."

The FBI agent pushed the man into the back of the car. As they were about to drive away, another car screeched into the parking area, and Agent Con Fox exited and went to Lissa.

"Don't worry. We will ensure you are safe. Welcome to the Chinese Tong gang. They are nasty and ruthless."

"I am scared. Can they find me?"

"We will make it very difficult for them to trace you. Have a little faith in what we will do to protect you."

"But I see on TV shows that these gangs often find people because certain police and FBI agents are crooked."

Agent Con Fox laughed.

"Lissa, do you think I am crooked? Those TV shows are all about drama. Yes, it has happened, but it is not as widespread as portrayed."

While they stood talking, an ambulance arrived to remove the body of the dead Chinese from the SUV.

"Lissa, I need you to take a close look at that SUV. Were there any distinguishing things about it that you remember? I need to establish that it was the one that caused that accident."

Lissa tried to recall what she had seen. Nothing came to mind.

"I am sorry, but there was nothing."

"Well, if you remember anything at all, please contact me directly. Are you OK to continue your drive from here to meet your friends? I want to be sure you are safe."

Lissa nodded and thanked him before climbing into her Jeep to complete her trip.

The balance of the drive was uneventful. She found the rustic lodge where her friends were waiting and celebrating their weekend away from responsibilities. Lissa parked in the guest area, pulled out her suitcase, and headed to join her friends. She was met at the door by effervescent Lucy.

"Lissa, you are finally here. What happened? What took so long?"

"Get me a glass of wine and I will tell you all."

The group sat in the lobby bar, sipping their wine and listening to Lissa describe the adventures of her trip. Lissa had finished her wine and looked up to find a server to order another glass. Her eyes scanned the room and stopped at the sight of a Chinese man in dark clothing staring at her. His face was grim, and his eyes, hard like flint, stared directly into hers. She stopped mid-sentence. The other girls looked at her and then turned to see what Lissa was staring at. The Chinese slowly turned and walked away.

Chapter 48

Hospital Events

The night at the Sonoma Valley Hospital passed quietly. Claude was in a deep sleep under the influence of the sedatives he had been administered. Barry had provided some comic relief to the nurses before he was anesthetized for his procedure. Buzz was not so fortunate. He lay in traction, his arm and leg in casts, the bone in his leg broken in several places.

Normal morning routines started with orderlies distributing breakfast to patients. Doctors walked the corridors, stopping at certain rooms to check on patients.

In Claude's room, the doctor looked over his chart and again examined it. After consulting with another doctor, he addressed Claude.

"You are very lucky. You suffered a mild concussion and avoided a major head injury. Based on what we see, you can be discharged, but we will want to do a follow-up in a couple of days."

"What about my business partner, Barry Jones? Can he be discharged?"

"His situation is a little more difficult. He has had minor surgery. We will need to check him later and determine whether he can be discharged."

In Barry's room, there was some hilarity. Due to the location of the surgery and sensitivity, he had been required to sleep with a large donut-shaped pillow beneath his rear. The nurses were required to sponge-clean him before the doctor's visit. The nurses were giggling and trying to be professional, but Barry was creating an impossible situation. As the nurses attempted to work, Barry broke into the Australian song, 'Tie me Kangaroo down, sport' that had been made famous around the world by the artist Rolf Harris. The meaning was not lost on the nurses, as they attempted to clean his private parts, a task complicated by his singing and their uncontrolled laughter.

The doctor walked in and stood frowning at the scene.

"Gidday, mate. How's it? These great nurses are doing a bonza job."

"Mr. Jones. We have protocols to adhere to. Please treat our staff with respect."

"Well, Doctor, it seems a little cheery singsong here is appreciated. Now, tell me, can I be discharged?"

The doctor requested Barry to roll over so he could examine where the parts of the tree splinters had been removed. He then checked the stitches tying together his split scrotum.

"It is probably better for you to stay here, but if you have somewhere to rest for the next few days, I see no reason to keep you here."

"Bloody great news. Doctor, where can I find the attaché case that was delivered to the hospital last night? It contains very important items."

"It is probably at security. Check before you are discharged in case it has been stored elsewhere."

An hour later, Claude, with his head bandaged, joined Barry, and together they went to sign out of the hospital. Barry retrieved the case.

"We need to rent a car and drive to the offices and get the systems protected before those criminals start anything."

" I called Marie-France this morning. I informed her of Buzz's condition and that he will be hospitalized for a week or more. She was hysterical and is flying from France to be with him."

"We need to get to the California offices as soon as we can and convene a meeting with our legal, investment bankers, and financial people. I am sure there will be police and representatives from the Securities Commission there as well. It will take a day before they arrive. We must waste no more time."

"I am going to call our offices, and they can send a car for us. It will be faster."

An hour later, they left the hospital for the de Passioné offices in Napa, but not before visiting Buzz, who was not happy.

"I need to know what SOBS did this to us. I will personally hunt them down and settle the score. Is the security device I brought to you safe?"

Claude and Barry assured Buzz that they had the device and to rest as they were leaving to deal with the problems created by the syndicate.

Two days passed. Buzz remained irritable. He was advised that Marie-France was traveling from France to be with him. It was some relief for him. He looked forward to her arrival to break the monotony.

It was mid-morning of the third day when Buzz realized something was happening at the hospital that wasn't normal. He watched nurses and orderlies running past the entrance to his room on their way to the hospital entrance. Many were laughing.

Marie-France had arrived in style.

She stood in front of the reception desk, demanding to see the Head Nurse. The receptionist stared at Marie-France, unable to speak or respond.

Marie-France was fully dressed in a 1950s nurse uniform. She wore the small nurse's cap on top of her teased jet-black hair, a full-length white pinafore, thick white stockings, white shoes, and cuffs. She has a stethoscope and a large crucifix hanging around her neck.

Staff stood looking at the sight, not daring to confront her.

"What are you all standing there for? I was a matron. Show some respect. I am here to nurse my husband, Buzz Kutz. Take me to him."

The on-duty Head Nurse walked forward and introduced herself. After the introductions, she escorted Marie-France to Buzz's room.

Marie-France howled when she saw Buzz. The nurse attempted to console her but failed. Instead, Marie-France barked orders.

"I am a nurse. I was a matron. Get a spare bed in here for me. Bring extra blankets and pillows. I am staying here and I will look after him. Get the doctor who is responsible for him. I need to speak to him immediately."

The young nurse in Buzz's room hesitated. The head nurse nodded for her to leave and arrange for the requested items.

She followed the young nurse from the room and signaled the security guard.

"I have agreed to let her stay in his room. She has a problem. I don't think she represents any risk, other than being annoying. Keep an eye on her."

For the rest of the day, Marie-France remained next to Buzz's bed. The hospital staff was kind to her, but couldn't help but joke about her.

Chapter 49

de Passioné Winery Offices, California.

The offices were active. Trucks arrived with the desks and chairs needed to set up the temporary conference room for the meeting with the investment bankers, lawyers, police forces, and others.

The attendees were arriving in the afternoon, and Claude and Barry checked to information packages. The newly generated financials and disclosures were included in the packages.

For the last day, Claude worked with the IT staff in France and California to set up the secure VPN. When it was operational and fully tested, he accessed the servers containing the databases for both the business and the family's personal information. He established new accounts with secure sites and built a new registry of data that was fully encrypted. He had asked for assistance from both the French and US Security intelligence to achieve the desired result. Finally, the data was safely migrated and is inaccessible to any third party.

Mid-afternoon, those representatives for the affected groups arrived. Invitations had been delivered to a few of the most important parties, and then under strict confidence. There were extreme steps taken to prevent knowledge of the meeting from reaching Tantamore Capital, the Arnie Jacobson Hedge Funds, or any of their associated affiliates. Claude had arranged a reception to allow each party to informally meet and feel welcome despite the difficult circumstances.

After a couple of hours, the representatives were directed to the conference and formally received by Claude. He advised the assembled that every person in attendance was to sign a full confidentiality agreement, as there were ongoing legal actions and the authorities in respective jurisdictions were concerned that their activities be kept secret. Claude also pointed out that the extreme penalties under the law should the information be leaked. The room was in total silence.

"I will start by saying we have secured our business files from the possible manipulation we understand is about to be attempted. Tomorrow morning, officials from law enforcement in the countries affected will address you and you will learn more about the intended attack on de Passioné. In the packages we had prepared by our legal and financial professionals, you will find the exact and correct information. I ask you to discard anything that you may have obtained from other sources. Tomorrow, you will be shown the extent to which a crime syndicate went to collapse de Passioné businesses and family holdings. We intend to be fully transparent and advise you to study the materials provided in those packages before tomorrow's meeting."

Claude stepped away from the lectern and was met by a small group. He deferred answering any questions.

He and Barry quietly slipped away from the gathered representatives.

"Well, Barry, tomorrow morning will be showtime. Let's hope all goes well tonight. It's one big gamble."

Barry looked at Claude and smiled at his appearance. He was dressed impeccably in a fine suit, yet with his bandaged head, he looked like a ninja warrior. Claude had a similar reaction to Barry's tender condition and saw him shuffling like a prematurely aged person.

"Let's go and sit in private and enjoy a fine wine before we visit the lodge for dinner". Barry agreed.

Sitting in a luxurious sales area of the offices, Claude requested one of the waiters hired for the event to bring him the wine, after which he sat and looked at Barry with concern.

"I am concerned that someone from those in attendance may leak some details and compromise the whole operation."

"I had thought about that risk as well. I do not think it would be to anyone's advantage. From what we know, the only people who stand to gain from our failure would be those in the syndicate. Everyone else stands to lose."

To ensure they had not overlooked anything, Claude and Barry reviewed the actions planned before leaving for the lodge.

Satisfied that everything had been addressed, Claude drove a company car to the lodge as Barry was still limited by his injury.

Upon arriving at the lodge, they were welcomed by the staff who immediately recognized Claude. The owner welcomed them and expressed concern over Claude's bandaged head and Barry's mobility.

"Charles, we are fine. Just had a little car mishap while driving up here. Please show us to a private table."

As they walked through the restaurant, Claude smiled as he watched a group of young ladies enjoying the evening. There were several empty wine bottles on their table, and the girls were laughing and chattering.

"Do you remember those days, Barry? Fun with friends and very few worries."

Charles, the owner, seated them at a corner table next to a window from which they had a view of the lighted gardens.

Once they had settled, Charles offered to take their drink order. Claude decided to select a wine from a neighboring winery. The winery had recently been sold to a young family, and he was curious about the quality of the wines they were producing. Charles was surprised by Claude's selection.

While waiting for the wine to be brought to the table, Claude looked around the restaurant, and that is when he saw a tall man dressed in a light grey suit arrive and sit at the table with the girls. He was convinced he knew the man from somewhere, but could not recall where.

The wine arrived, and Claude performed the tasting. He was impressed. The waiter recited a few specials for that evening. Claude ordered Escargot au Gratin and a main course of local venison. Barry decided on potato soup followed by a porterhouse steak done medium with a side of fresh asparagus, a baked potato topped with sour cream, fresh chives, and ground bacon bits.

"Claude, I think we are fortunate in that Marie-France decided to stay near Buzz at the hospital. It would have been difficult with her at the meeting tomorrow. As much as I like your mother, she can create some of the more interesting situations in life."

Their meals arrived. Claude was amazed. The quality exceeded his expectations.

They ate in silence, and Claude continued to glance at the table where the young women were celebrating. He was certain he knew the man. While he was watching, the man stood to assist one of the women to stand up from her chair and leave the table. She walked toward Claude's table and headed to the washrooms. Curiosity got the better of Claude. As she passed, he raised his hand.

"Excuse me. My name is Claude. I was wondering who the man sitting with you at the table is. I know his face and cannot place it. It is driving me crazy."

Lissa looked back at the table and then replied.

"Oh, that's FBI Special Agent Con Fox. He was in the area and is joining us for drinks."

"I knew it. Say Hi to him for me."

When Lissa was gone, Claude spoke with Barry.

"I assume he is here for the meeting tomorrow. I am getting the feeling it is going to be one very interesting morning."

Chapter 50

Morning Glory

Cars, limousines, and official-looking SUVs started pulling into the de Passioné winery parking area. Valets handed the drivers a receipt and drove the vehicles to a guarded compound that had been set up at the request of the local security officials. Armed agents stood at the entrances to the building. Security was tight, and each person entering was validated. Nothing was left to chance.

Claude and Barry were advised to wait until given direction before starting the meeting, and that a special group would be arriving to address the meeting first. They were also informed that the group would be accompanied by a special media and news team.

They were not given the option to object. The directives were given by high-ranking US Military officers who were accompanied by official US Secret Service plainclothes security officers.

Attendees continued to arrive until 10 minutes before the scheduled start of the meeting. There were far more attendees than Claude expected. Additional seating was installed. Minutes before the scheduled start, Claude went to the lectern to address the assembly.

"Good morning, all. I hope everyone who stayed over in the area last evening had an enjoyable time. I am requested by officials from the US State Department to delay the meeting for a few minutes pending the arrival of certain officials who will address you all."

A murmur and some grumbling spread through the crowd.

"I am assured they will be here soon, and they expect to make a short statement, after which there will be the option for some questions."

As he finished speaking, a small convoy of cars and SUVs drove into the property and directly to the entrance doors. The doors were opened by men dressed in full military dress who saluted the occupants as they exited. A line of officials entered the building and took positions on the stage behind the lectern and microphone. A second vehicle, a pickup truck with a mounted satellite dish and bristling with antennae, sped into the grounds. The doors flew open, and men equipped with TV Cameras rushed into the entrance. Two females carrying portable microphones followed.

The officials were introduced to Claude and Barry and then proceeded to take their respective positions on the stage, and waited for the TV news team to ready itself.

"Good morning, all. I am General Vince Johnson with the US State Department. I am here this morning to announce the successful completion of coordinated actions taken by our allies. These actions were in response to the de Passioné crisis and others. I am sure after we present the situation and actions, you will all understand the impact on de Passioné and the meeting that is to follow. I will now hand over to Colonel Mick Stutz of Homeland Security."

"Thank you, General. What had started and appeared to be a commercial squabble over a French business turned out to be a lot more. The events at de Passioné resulted in an investigation by DGCE, the French External Security Force. The findings uncovered the existence of a major international crime syndicate. As a French-owned industry was threatened. The DGSE shared the information with other countries that were involved due to the criminal activities of individuals and companies based in those countries. As a result, the British MI5 played a major role, which will become evident a little later. Interpol has played an invaluable role. The French Security Forces, DGE, and DGSI were both instrumental. The Italian Guardia di Finanza, the US FBI, and the US Department of the Treasury, The FBI, and in China, we are working with the Ministry of State Security. The cooperation between all these forces has been exceptional.

What started as an investigation into peculiar events at the de Passioné winery led to a deeper investigation at the request of management. Part of that investigation resulted in a forensic audit undertaken by Mr. Horatio Henderson and his team. This led to the discovery of unorthodox financial transactions that diluted the true values of the company. Additionally, that audit stumbled into further transactions performed by two large financial institutions here in the States and one in the OK. In the States, investigations uncovered highly illegal activities performed by the Arnie Jacobson Hedge Funds, while in the UK, similar activities were discovered for Tanatamore Capital. Activities that, when investigated, led to the money laundering of funds from drug operations in Italy and a questionable investment from a well-known supplier of drugs from China.

A coordinated and synchronized raid was undertaken earlier today, and multiple arrests have been made. There will be a detailed press conference later today, and representatives from the different jurisdictions will address the press and answer questions.

There has been a lot of speculation regarding the disappearance of Claude de Passioné while these investigations were happening. I wish to end any speculation. Claude was abducted and held captive, during which time he was drugged and incapacitated. He was rescued by an elite French special force, for which we are grateful.

Over the coming weeks, there will be disclosures relating to the efforts of that crime syndicate and their attempts to sabotage businesses in different countries. The method was simple and easy for those with trusted systems to implement. First, they disrupted suppliers and then attacked the finances of the target company to force financial and contractual defaults. From early analysis, Arnie Jacobson Hedge Funds funneled the drug money to different parties, and Tantamore Capital executed the trades and actions that would cause the failure of the companies, after which they financed operations to buy the remnants for pennies on the dollar. I now pass this over to Claude de Passioné, a man who should be congratulated for his tenacity in saving the company and your investments. Claude, if you please.

The assembled group clapped loudly as Claude went to the lectern.

Chapter 51

2 Months later

de Passioné Chateau, France

Claude and Barry sat on the rear garden patio overlooking the floral masterpiece of a garden. The frequent media requests regarding his capture and the planned sabotage of the family businesses had died down. Life for the family had a semblance of normalcy. Claude was enjoying his life, but found his mind wandering back to his life in Rarotonga in the Cook Islands. He missed certain aspects of life there, but not as much as he missed his daughter, Peace.

In the pool, Buzz walked back and forth exercising his recently healed leg. Now and then, he would walk over to the side to rest and take a sip of the gin and tonic that Marie-France kept refreshed for him. He had made a decision. He decided that the wine and spirits business was too rough and rugged for him and devoted his time to growing his aviation business. He enjoyed flying his executive clients to exotic locations in his private jet.

Marie-France lay in a hammock reading the latest Ocean Divers Monthly magazine. Still searching for adventures, she has joined a deep-sea diving club and enrolled to travel to far-off locations to dive on shipwrecks.

Yvette and Fleur worked at the patio table, refining the menu for the Bistro they had jointly opened under the name 'Petit Fleur." The locals and tourists loved the Bistro, and reservations were hard to get.

Fleur had moved in with Claude after he had invited her and her father, Pierre Leclair, to visit the winery and spend a week with him and his family. Fleur saw Claude differently. He was not suffering the effects of the incarceration or the frequent drugging he had endured. She saw an even stronger man, and her love for him grew. She was continuing her university education remotely.

Yvette nursed Bruce, the new baby, on her knee while she worked with Fleur. Bruce was the apple of Barry's eye. His world rotated around the baby.

Claude looked at the time on his Cartier watch. It was almost time for his visitors to arrive. He had invited the FBI Special Agent and his partner, Lissa, to the Chateau for dinner. Lissa had been a key witness to the accident caused by the Chinese Tong gang. Had they killed him, the de Passioné business would have collapsed. Her witness statement resulted in the arrests of several key members of the gang in San Francisco.

While he waited, his mind drifted back to Vick Spagnoli and Sir Reginald Coxburn. With the arrests and investigations, the true leader of the syndicate had been identified…The Boss, as she was called….Lady Agnes Thwacker. Sir Reginald was a front…her lapdog. She was unlikely to see freedom again. The charges against her, if proven, would lock her away for years.

Claude smiled. Finally, there was a peace he had been seeking for years. The turmoil of his life was gone, and a calmness soothed away the sad and troubled events of the past. Life was finally treating him well….or so he believed.

FIN

The Story's Characters

Where are they now??

Claude de Passioné is still in charge of the company and family.

Marie-France… Enrolled in International deep-sea diving courses.

Barry Jones…Madly in love with Yvette, his wife, and a new baby.

Buzz Kuttz…Operating his air charter and crop dusting businesses.

Sir Reginald Coxburn… Died of syphilis 1 month after the trial began.

Lady Agnes Thwacker….committed suicide.

Arrnie Jacobson…serving 25 years in jail for fraud, money laundering, and security violations.

Knuckles O'Brien..gave up crime and joined a monastery.

Vicky Spaginoli…died destitute and never recovered.

Luigi Fratti… protected by corrupt Italian police and politicians, expanded his empire.

Lee Chang..found with his throat cut in Guangdong Province.

Horatio Henderson… died of boredom as an accountant.

Fleur Leclair is in love with Claude. Opened a Bistro with Yvette.

Lissa… witnessed the assassination attempt. Moved under a witness protection plan to live anonymously in the Caribbean.